Rupert Pinter

and the

Curse of the Tuatha De Danann

ROBERT NC THOMAS

Copyright © 2012 Robert NC Thomas

All rights reserved.

ISBN: 1479122564
ISBN-13: 978-1479122561

DEDICATION

To the Four Guys:

The Actor, The Singer, The Soldier, The Teacher

ACKNOWLEDGMENTS

Robert Durbin for providing the perfect template for villainy. Andrew Richards for joining me around the world. Alex Calvin for friendly competition and support. Steph Bates for the first honest proofread; and Darren Freebury-Jones for the sparrows tears that followed.

My amazing Nicky for the cover design and not letting me forget this. The History Departments of both Llanishen High School and Cardiff University for giving me the drive and resources to contemporise Pinter's adventures. The minds of Lucas and Spielberg for showing that adventure never ages, and my Dad for introducing me to the genre that shaped my childhood.

Thank you all.

Rob Thomas, January 2013

DANGER IN THE AIR

The air was burning his lungs trying to escape and Pinter knew he was running out of time. He hadn't had a chance to take a breath before Lawrence had locked his hands around his throat. Realising it was now or never, with Herculean effort he shoved Lawrence backwards, catching him on the wrong foot and swinging the two of them in an arc - directly into the steam rushing through the hole in the pipe beside them.

The shriek was horrific, as Lawrence's skin cooked violently through the thin black shirt he wore. He threw Pinter off him, sending him sprawling to the ground of the previously impassable part of the tunnel.

Clear of the steam.

Lawrence staggered with searing flesh behind the screen of hot air, caught as though he were a marionette puppet of the Hunchback of Notre Dame lit from behind. There was a clatter as he collapsed to the ground, moaning in excruciating pain as his body roasted.

Pinter shrugged off the shock, wiping sweat from his brow and breathing in fresh air deeply. It struck him that the purchase of a new tuxedo for the event was a serious mistake. The sleeves were already stained with oil and the lapels were starting to furrow.

He shook his head clear of vain sartorial thoughts and looked ahead of him. There was only one way to go, and that was onwards and upwards. He stepped up to the ladder and grabbed the first rung.

"Well," he muttered to himself. "Here goes nothing."

ROBERT NC THOMAS

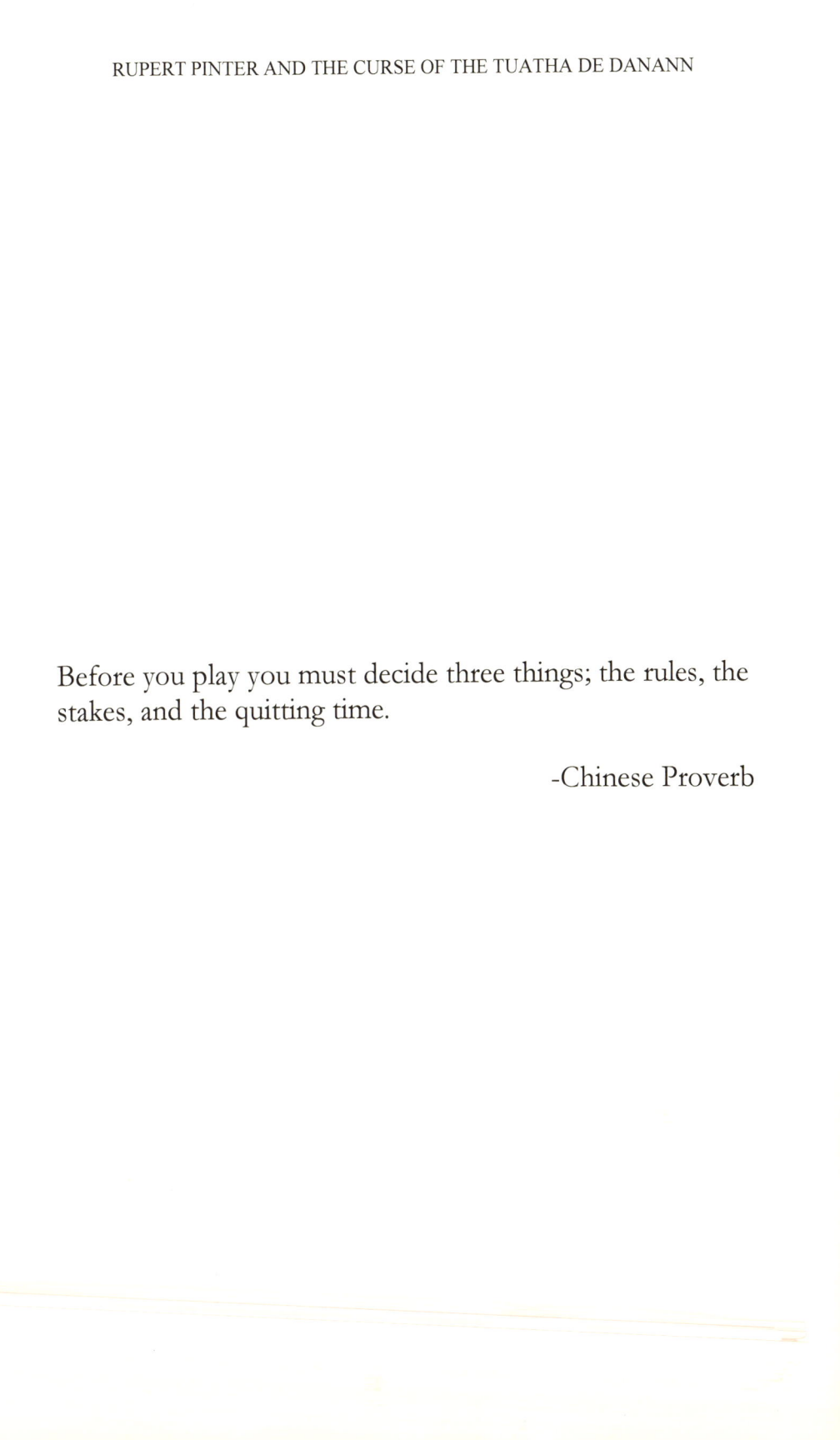

Before you play you must decide three things; the rules, the stakes, and the quitting time.

-Chinese Proverb

ROBERT NC THOMAS

ONE

The Welsh Mountains
JANUARY, 1932

A fresh winter morning mist hung like a blanket in the air, earthly and strangely foreboding. Crushing frost beneath worn leather work boots as he emerged from his tent, Harry Lester mashed a panama hat onto his thick mass of black hair and gazed up at the dawn sun creeping over the mountains. The sky was painted with magnificent blues, purples and reds and the moon still hung in the sky, a ghostly sphere clinging to the whisps of cirrus clouds. Training his ear above the splash of the river that tore past the encampment, he heard the soft whistle of early birds rising to catch worms.

Lester yawned heavily, stretching his arms out in a vain effort to shake off another uncomfortable night's sleep in a military-issue cot. His attempt failed miserably, as it did every morning. Instead he resorted to twisting his head from side to side in an attempt to soothe his sore, ravaged neck. He'd foolishly assumed, when he took up his place sharing a tent with a snoring Chinese exchange student, that he would have grown accustomed to the cramped, cold quarters of the expedition. As for all 19 year olds, though, this was certainly not the case. The sense of adventure that had filled him when he signed up at the end of Dr. Randle's British Prehistory seminar was dulled by the first week of relentless digging. Foraging in the ground for Celtic-this and Prehistoric-that was hardly the romantic adventure that Lester had read so often about. Here he stood at the back end of the month long dig, all the more grateful to be heading home - to be away from the tools and pits that filled other students with an interest he couldn't even begin to fathom. He was sure that there was more to archaeology than looking at shards of ancient pottery, but now that certainty was hard to find. Each morning he woke considering dropping the module of study altogether. Now he longed to be back in the confines of the Daggers Club in Oxford, amongst his *true* peers, sipping whiskey over ice with soda and adjusting his dickie-bow in the warmth beside the drawing room fire as they discussed the cricket results. Now he longed to be far away from the fingers of cold Welsh air that grazed his neck through his open collar all day.

The camp was near empty. A handful of tents littered the floor of the valley. The closed flaps added to the atmosphere of serenity. They were miles from the nearest village, let alone the nearest town. Their campsite was off the beaten track – so much so that a makeshift wooden bridge had been hastily constructed to cross the river without the risk of being carried away. Though the current was barely noticeable when looking at the river, it was startlingly strong - all it would take was a slip on a rock to tumble into the drink and find yourself remerging a mile downstream with a bruised ego and a mild case of hypothermia.

This early in the morning it didn't surprise Lester that most of his archaeologically inclined peers had yet to stir from their slumbers. His tent companion continued to snore. The heavy, raspy breathing seemed impossibly loud – louder than the waterfall that lay nearby. It seemed even more inconceivable that for the last four weeks Lester had managed to get any sort of semblance of sleep at all, but nevertheless, when the body demanded rest, the mind would eventually give in - no matter how loud the disturbance.

Lester shook his head clear of bleary-eyed wonderings. He had a job to do, and pulling the brim of his hat low against the chill of the morning breeze, he stepped towards the tent of Doctor Geoffrey Randle, sweeping the heavy canvas flap to one side and ducking under the canopy into the warmth of the professor's inner sanctum. The air was ripe with the sweet scent of pipe smoke and Earl Grey tea heating in a kettle beside a camp-bed. The old man was leaning back in his chair. His bootless feet were up on the work table as he polished a revolver, and he didn't so much as glance up before addressing Lester directly: "Morning Harry. Would you like a cup of tea?"

Lester nodded: "I'd love one."

"Good man. The kettle is still warm, so help yourself." Randle nodded to a trio of mugs that sat beside the bed. "They're all clean. Don't be shy, there's plenty to go around."

"Thank you, sir."

Satisfied with the cleanliness of the revolver, the old

man grinned to himself and slipped it back into its holster. Then, in an extravagant motion, he swept his socks from the table and dropped his feet into his filthy leather boots. "Are you ready?"

"Certainly, sir."

"Good man. What about Pinter? Is he about?"

Lester felt a wave of jealousy dash through him. "Haven't seen him yet this morning, sir."

"Shame. I'm sure he'll be around shortly." Randle grabbed a wide-brimmed Australian hunting hat and placed it carefully onto his head, adjusting the pinch and brim as he did so. "His father was the same, y'know. Useless at early starts. Didn't bode well really, particularly considering he was a doctor on call."

He was a jovial old man, mused Lester, with the kindly eyes of a much younger fellow. They held the glisten of childhood excitement. It was odd, but in a particularly noticeable way the professor seemed to have aged more rapidly in the last few weeks than he had in the entire previous semester at Oxford. Perhaps it was the prominence of flecks of grey in the bushy beard that covered his chin.

Lester could only assume that it was directly linked to a nasty piece of business involving one of the senior members of the Faculty of History. Nicholas Tirey and Geoffrey Randle had been close. Randle had studied under the former for many years at Oxford before taking up a teaching position there himself. They had entered a brotherly union on the battlefields of the Great War, the sort of union that was truly made to last. It seemed to most who were within the inner circles of Oxford University that their student-teacher bond was infallible, and whisperings in lecture theatres suggested that the only reason Randle launched the expedition to Wales was to finish a project that his mentor had started. Some thought that Tirey was only hanging around because he wanted to see Randle retire first. Nicholas Tirey was ancient. His death was hardly untimely. That didn't make it any less suspicious, though.

Lester sipped gently at his tea as Randle laced up his boots and swung his gun belt around his waist, his eyes pausing for a moment on a cane that sat near the door. Lester was aware of Randle's occasional use of a walking stick, but the youthful vigor that had come upon the man appeared to render the cane useless. Satisfied by his routine, one that had been practiced for many years, in many countries, but always with the same impeccable result, Randle grinned wildly: "Shall we go and make history?"

Lester nodded, replacing the empty mug, and followed the professor out of the tent. They started immediately towards the waterfall that crashed down a few score paces away from their tents. Despite the proximity, the other students in the camp hadn't uttered a word of complaint, and all seemed to consider the river that ran past the encampment on its long, winding path down the mountain soothing – particularly after long hours of numbing excavation. But that was the name of the game with archaeology: a lot of work and not much to show for it. Far too many times, Lester had been tempted to keep a piece of ancient jewelry if he found it, but the chance would have been a fine thing. It seemed to him that they were digging in the wrong place. Only as the expedition drew to a close did he realise that it was the waterfall that they had come for, or rather what lay beyond it. The other work taking place was mere distraction. He felt a fool to have wasted time as he had, digging and entrenching and sifting through the dirt looking for Neolithic burial practices that simply didn't exist.

As they approached the falls, Randle's eyes lit up. Lester hadn't seen beyond the threshold yet, but Randle had, and Harry knew only too well that whatever lay behind the wall of crashing water was beyond his teacher's wildest dreams.

"Good morning!"

The voice came from a ridge above them, and Lester glanced over to see the boyish good-looks of a khaki-clad Rupert Pinter approaching down the gentle incline that led into the forest. He was 18, a year younger than Lester, of a normal build with floppy blond hair and a face that suggested he was considerably younger than he was. Atop his work shirt he wore dark brown braces, and he too had a gun-belt slung about his waist, a Webley revolver tucked into the holster. Lester couldn't help but despise him, but not just for his charming good looks, but rather the over-confidence that came with them. In any other situation they would have moved in completely different circles, but Pinter's looks masked a great deal of intelligence and wit, and made him a regular hoot at the Dagger Club whenever he had the sense to put on a cravat and dress like a gentleman for once. The boy was lucky his father was such a well respected physician before his death, otherwise Oxford as a university of choice would have been out of the question. Morbidly, Lester wished that that had been entirely the case for Pinter.

He crossed the wooden bridge and sidled up alongside them: "Morning, Harry! How are you?"

"Fine. Where the devil have you been?" Lester tried to be as short and rude as possible without drawing any attention to himself, instead masking his festering dislike of Pinter behind faux-sarcastic scorn.

"Short walk. Worth it in this weather. Y'know, if you follow the path all the way to the top there is a fantastic view of the sunrise. It creeps over the trees on the horizon as if it's scared of appearing at all. Makes you wonder what the Neoliths thought of it all. I've made a habit of it now with a flask of tea in the morning. Might as well, especially considering the snoring coming from your tent, Harry." Harry cringed with embarrassment to himself at the implication as Pinter looked to Randle: "Are we set?"

Randle nodded and tossed a lantern his way. Fumbling, Pinter caught it clumsily, and Lester couldn't help but feel content with the knowledge that Rupert had very noticeable flaws. Pinter simply grinned at him, shrugged, and went about adjusting the brown flat cap that he'd perched on top of the mass of blond.

They fixed their gazes firmly on the waterfall. The valley seemed to close in around it, moss-strewn walls arching to the sky, shutting off all the light as the morning sun fought to illuminate the damning entrance to their underground prison. Above them, the canopy of trees that jutted out at morbid angles seemed to reach together, grasping at each other like bony hands. Spikes of water hung from the plant life, lending the impression that the jaws of hell were about to swallow them up. They were a good 150 paces from the camp now, and the intensity of the water here increased dramatically – a maelstrom whipping the river to a frenzied speed despite the enormous size of the splash pool they were circumnavigating, which sucked in the output of the falls and belched it into oblivion. The froth kicked back as it struck the surface, creating a towering cloud of white water - the womb which they were about to crawl into.

"Right then," Randle murmured, as he snapped the lamp in his hand on in a quick and fluid motion. "Shall we?"

TWO

The trio clambered wordlessly up a ledge and hoisted themselves into the cavern. The cave hidden behind the falls was dank and formidable. The crash of cascading water echoed in the seemingly endless void that lay before them – a deafening cacophony that threw itself from wall to wall and back upon them and which made even their loudest shouts impossible to discern. The three walked in silence, heading deeper into the unknown, the weak flickering of the small lanterns guiding their way through rocks that in the pale yellow light looked like sharp fangs.

Pinter couldn't help but murmur to himself: "I forget, do stalagmites go up, or down?" He wasn't expecting an answer but posed the question nonetheless, hoping to break that miserable silence that had fallen between them. His words were lost in the sound of the falls behind them, so he shrugged to himself and whispered: "Something to find out when we get home then, I suppose?"

A peculiar, ghostly mist hung about them – the

combination of the spray from the waterfall behind them doubling back on itself and the grey steam of their breaths in the deathly cold. The wraith-like shapes were too human for Pinter's liking as they swirled into nothingness, and he felt goose-bumps rise on his skin as they began to arch skyward. Despite himself, he gripped his lantern tighter in an attempt to find warmth, hoping to find solace in the belief that it was simply the cold creating the awful sting of trepidation in his belly.

Eventually Randle drew them to a halt. Ahead of them lay a junction. One path lead down an incline and further into the darkness beyond. Both Lester and Pinter shared a hope that it wasn't going to be their destination. The other seemed to be a trough-like bank of an underground river, that vanished beneath their feet into another tunnel and which ebbed against their path, occasionally spilling over and trickling back to the entrance or down into the depths of the cave before them.

On second thoughts, mused Pinter, *maybe the first option wouldn't be too bad after all.*

The way the water moved suggested that the flow continued below them, presumably emerging beneath the torrent of water in the splash pool now far behind. The river seemed to stretch into the dark recesses beyond, far out of sight.

Randle nodded to the direction of the other path and Pinter and Lester followed him as the sound of the waterfall grew distant. Soon they noticed they could speak without raising their voices.

The first sound they were able to make out was an agreeable whistling. Randle seemed to be keeping his mind occupied with a tune from Bizet's *Carmen*. Eventually, the hurried voice of their teacher broke through the acoustics of the cave:

"You wouldn't think it, but these tunnels run for miles!" Randle seemed on the verge of a heart-attack with exhilaration. "You could easily go missing down here. People have. Local legend tells of farmers from centuries ago who went looking for lost sheep in here and never came back. So stay close, boys. I've got the map!"

He waved a frayed piece of parchment towards them, and with a tinge of sadness, he shouted: "If Tirey is right about this, then maybe he didn't die in vain!"

Neither Pinter nor Lester knew how to reply. The recent death had left everyone shaken. The mumblings of foul play had everyone on edge. Pinter didn't doubt for a moment that Randle had only the purest intentions of honouring his friend's memory, but questions *would* be asked. Especially when they considered Randle's acquisition of the map. A nervous Tirey had mailed it to him the day before he died without any sort of explanation. His legacy was a scruffy piece of material.

It struck Pinter there was something much more sinister afoot than a simple motoring accident.

For the first time, he had a chance to take in his surroundings properly. The shadows of stalagmites cast eerie bone-shaped silhouettes on the walls and as they walked the shadows danced as if caught in an eternal waltz. The cobwebs that hung from all corners of the rock looked like capes and dresses flowing in the pulse of a serenade.

"They call this the Passage of the Dancers," Randle started, noticing Pinter's awed expression. "They say the shadows that dance in these caves are the ghosts of hunters who found themselves trapped in this oblivion forever. There are tales of men who ventured into these tunnels, never to be seen again, becoming another dancer, wallowing for all eternity in a morbid waltz. Whether or not what lies beyond the dancers is common knowledge is another matter, however. As I said, no-one has ever returned, and for our sake, we should hope not. In the strictest professional sense, I mean, of course. We shouldn't want to come all this way to find that our prize has already been claimed by a grave-robber now, would we?"

"What exactly are we looking for?" Pinter asked.

"The Dagda Cauldron."

There was a long pause between them. Pinter had heard the name, and it rang a bell quite prominently in the back of his mind but he couldn't quite place it. Lester, on the other hand, and with evident delight, was keen to jump in with an answer: "The Four Treasures myth?"

"Exactly."

"Wait a second," the cogs in Pinter's mind began to fly. "Four Treasures? The Druids? That's Celtic Mythology, isn't it?"

"Correct." Randle seemed pleased, Lester less so. "The Dagda Cauldron was supposedly one of the Four Treasures of the Tuatha De Danann, brought with them to Ireland. It's a variation on the Bible's book of Exodus, I suppose, if you want a comparison. The Tuatha De journeyed from the four corners of the Earth, finally settling in Ireland. If Tirey was correct, and if his research stands up, we're on track to recovering solid evidence of occult practices. He seemed to think that the legends telling of the emergence and the fall of the Tuatha De Danann have some sort of merit."

"How do you mean?" Pinter asked, without even thinking.

"Legend tells that after the fall of the Tuatha De Danann, three Druid priests fled to Britain, each in possession of a sacred object – one of the four treasures. The four treasures that the Tuatha De, who were the founding fathers of Ireland, had brought with them in their exodus to their new land. What these priests found before when they reached the British Isles was an uncultured land, unlearned in the arts of philosophy, tradition and magic. A barbaric land of cannibal practice and burial rites that they found obscene, particularly after decades...perhaps even millennia, of honing their skills in the dark arts. Comparing the mythology with the archaeological evidence, the early Britons were simply primitive by the standards of the Tuatha De. They knew that these people, who we can *assume* were the Neolithic Britons, had no right to wield such powers as they had in their possession, and so each took it upon himself to secure the treasure he held for all eternity, until the day the Tuatha De Danann would return to claim the objects they once held so dear."

"You said four treasures. That accounts for three that reached the British Isles. What happened to the last?"

"The Stone of Fal, Rupert. It was always destined to remain in Ireland and scream and shriek when touched by the true king of the land. Call it a beacon, if you will, guiding the Tuatha De Danann home." He snorted then, breaking the mood considerably. "If you believe that sort of thing. For skeptics like me, this sort of expedition is a jump into the unknown. I suppose, really, it's a question of whether you'd feel the need to believe it yourself or not, Pinter. Well?"

"I don't know what I believe, but I know I wouldn't like to cross the divine. As far as I'm concerned, we have no right to question what we will never know much about."

"Then you should open your mind, Pinter," Randle grinned. "Strange things happen. They happen all the time. If we don't question the divine, how are we human?"

They rounded a corner and the claustrophobia of the passage became unbearable as the tunnel shrank. The three could only walk in single file, with Randle in the lead and Pinter bringing up the rear. Eventually, the inevitable happened and they collided with a bump. Randle, who had been whistling quietly to himself and stringing a melodic line against the brash percussion of their footsteps echoing off the walls, fell silent. He stepped forward slowly, revealing to them as he did the massive cavern ahead. It was bathed in an eerie yellow light, sending the shadow of a skeleton that sat ahead towering above them.

Clutched in the arms of the skeletal figure was a glistening black cauldron. It looked brand new. Lunar and solar symbols covered the walls, and Pinter felt his breath escape as he took in the cavern with a feeling of pure astonishment.

Lester's eyes were wide: "That's it!"

"Don't move." Randle's words were cold, collected. All the joviality had gone from his voice.

"Why not? C'mon!"

Randle threw his arm out: "Harry, stop!"

It was far too late. Stepping beyond the threshold, Lester made it a matter of footsteps before his heel depressed a section of the floor and the ground fell away beneath him. Pinter and Randle could only watch wide-eyed as with a blood-curdling scream Lester vanished below them and onto the jagged spikes of rock that cushioned his descent. The fall was short but deadly, and Lester was dead on impact.

"Oh dear." Randle broke the silence, his voice punctuated more with genuine surprise than concern.

"Poor Harry."

"I dread to think of the paperwork."

There was a moment between them that seemed to last for a lifetime, and which gave Pinter a chance to assess the environment. The floor was made up of the fake, breakaway slabs that had seen the end of Lester, and evidently quite a few others, all patterned with individual representations of the symbols that appeared on the walls. What Pinter noticed, however, was the main difference. Where the slabs on the floor seemed to be randomly patterned, the wall showed a structured repetition.

A sequence of symbols.

"This is hopeless," Randle sighed as he started for the way they'd come. "Tirey made no reference of these. Not even a suggestion. The risk of this isn't worth it."

"Why *would* he make a reference to it?" Pinter allowed a boyish grin. "The writing is on the wall."

Randle shot him a quizzical look, but as Pinter motioned to the floor, the old man's eyes glistened: "Well done, boy!"

It took Pinter a moment to pluck up the courage to step forward. He knew only too well that one mistake would be his last. What if he was wrong about the symbols? What if they really meant nothing?

He shook his head clear of doubt. The first symbol was a waxing moon, and the appropriate slab seemed to grin sardonically at him as he approached. He swallowed heavily and stepped forward.

The ground held firm.

From behind him, the sound of Randle's sigh of relief was loud enough to reverberate through the entire chamber. The professor's voice was strained now as he called out the next in the sequence: "Rising sun!"

Stepping diagonally, Pinter's foot brushed against a symbol of a full moon, and he could feel the stone begin to crumble. He found his balance on the rising sun slab just as the moon fell away, vanishing to the jagged rocks below.

"That was close..."

"Concentrate, Rupert!"

Pinter shrugged the remark off as his eyes circled the

wall, looking for the next step in the pattern.

"Waning moon!" The shouts met his ears as his eyes met the pictograph.

"These things look too similar."

"I'm well aware!"

"Are you sure it's the right one?"

"As sure as I can be."

"Easy for you to say," he muttered under his breath as he scanned the floor for the lunar image. This time there was no room for a mistake – the slab was quite a stretch away, and even that was being generous. Pinter sucked in a breath and readied himself. After this, there was only one more to go. After this he'd made it more than halfway.

He stepped out, beads of sweat running from his temple to his nose.

Randle held his breath.

With the grace of a ballroom dancer, Pinter landed on the slab, which held firm. The relief rushed out of him.

"One more to go, Rupert!" Randle scanned the pattern, aiming to be certain: "Looks like sunset!"

"They didn't aim for clarity when they constructed this, did they?" Pinter yelled back, his teasing tinged with apprehension.

"I imagine assisting grave-robbers wasn't really high on their agenda. I doubt they ever expected us to get this far...you should be proud of yourself!"

Pinter forced himself to grin again, seeing the setting sun stone slab directly ahead. On second thoughts, this was all too easy. With an air of confidence he walked purposefully forward.

He felt the air escape his lungs and the terror rush through his blood as the slab collapsed beneath him.

THREE

"Rupert!"

Pinter clutched onto the solid ground ahead of him for dear life, hanging by his fingertips over the deadly abyss below. The strain was unbearable and wasn't helped by the bruising he'd received on the fall. His arms felt like they were on fire, and he screwed up his face in effort as he focused on getting back to safety. His legs kicked powerlessly below him and he felt his fingers start to ache. He couldn't hold on much longer.

Oh, great, he thought. *What a way to start a morning.*

"Rupert! Are you alright?"

Randle released a heavy sigh of relief as a voice, timid and pitched with strain, shouted back: "I think that was the wrong one!"

Pinter dragged himself out of the breach, his face crimson with struggle as he did so, and rolled onto the safe patch of ground in the centre of the chamber. He allowed himself a moment to catch his breath and looked back into the chasm below. Darkness met his eyes, an endless emptiness. As he squinted, trying to see the bottom, far below him he could see the glisten of water bouncing off jagged rocks in the feeble light from the chamber. The spikes closer to the chamber walls had given way to sloping gulf - a perilous drop indeed. "Jesus..."

His heart was racing now, beating mercilessly against his chest as though trying to escape his rib-cage, and he turned to face the prize.

The hollow eyes of the skeleton burrowed into him, searching his soul. The jaw was locked into a death-laugh, a gruesome portrait of eternal expiration. Skin had long rotted away from the bones, which looked as though they would turn to dust if he touched them. Scraps of rags hung loosely from the shoulders, clothes worn away by the ravages of time.

Perhaps a guardian left behind, he considered. *Glad I didn't have that job.*

Crouching before the macabre statue, Pinter ran his fingers gently through the air around the cauldron. It gave off a curiously electric aura, and for the first time it struck Pinter that there was something otherworldly about it. Something not meant to be. A shiver ran up his spine. All at once, he didn't want to touch it.

"Well go on then, boy! Get it and bring it back!"

Pinter looked back at Randle, who was wide-eyed and mystified by the object so close to their custody. The professor seemed to be salivating at the thought of such a find. He obviously couldn't feel the raw power of this...*thing*.

Turning his attention back to the skeletal figure, something in the darkest recesses of the hollow eye sockets seemed to grin mockingly. In the pit of his stomach he felt a wrenching. A strange sort of fear.

"I've got a nasty feeling about this."

Only Pinter heard himself as he muttered. He reached out and clasped his hands around the cauldron, slowly and gently lifting it free from the claws of the skeleton. The black, untarnished metal smoldered with warmth, and for the first time Pinter noticed a parchment tucked inside the ancient artifact. He withdrew it slowly, each movement in fear of damaging the archaic scroll.

If the parchment is this old, Pinter wondered to himself, *how can the cauldron look brand new?*

He took a quick look at the scroll. It seemed to be some sort of map, but the ancient Celtic inscriptions made no sense. The language was alien, different from anything he'd seen before. It appeared to depict a coastline, but he couldn't determine where. Off the coast was a small island. Though he couldn't understand the characters, it was clear that the island had some sort of significance. But where on Earth could it be, and what on Earth could it mean?

It didn't make any sense at all, but then, he didn't expect it to. He was robbing a skeleton, after all.

From beyond there came a low rumble, eerily similar to the sound of water being released and gaining great speed. Pinter looked down at the ground, watching rubble shift as the room trembled. Dust fell from the roof, showering him with powder. With a hiss, the skeleton fell to pieces, everything except the head turning instantly to a pile of dust. Then, suddenly, the skull rocketed to the ceiling in the pillar of a huge geyser of brown, icy water that burst from beneath the throne. Pinter fell back in shock, almost tumbling into the pit in surprise. As the water hit the low roof and spat down rain, Pinter threw the cauldron full force to Randle, who caught it, fumbling as he pulled the artifact in close to his chest.

The gap between the platform he stood on and the

nearest safe floor slab wasn't a distance he thought he could clear, but with nothing else for it and seeing no other choice, Pinter took a running jump and crashed down onto the edge of the slab. Slipping, he found himself sprawled on his chest as his legs dragged him backwards. His arms creaking with strain, he had to force himself to scramble back to his feet as icy water rained down on him. It was as though a storm had opened up in the confines of the cave, and he knew with horror that this kind of storm would have no surrender. The torrent was relentless. Wearily, Pinter dragged himself to his feet.

Leaping to the stones he knew were safe, within moments he was once again beside Randle, and they took off back up the passage, their feet slipping on the mud and rocks as the water behind them left the lake it had formed and started bubbling up the tunnel. As if taunting them, Lester's blood-stained Panama hat was astride the bubbling surge as it rose towards them. The corpse was lost, clearly tangled in the spikes, where Harry Lester would remain forever entombed.

As would they, if they didn't hurry.

"Move, boy!" Randle was frantically pressing forward, the light from his lamp swinging wildly and barely giving them enough illumination to see their way forward.

"I'm coming, go!"

They ran as fast as they could back the way they'd come, forced into single file as the cavern became constricted. Their legs were ablaze with pain as they hit the incline back to the Passage of the Dancers. For the first time since they'd set off from the camp, Rupert noticed that Randle was limping. It was odd, as though the impending doom that surrounded them brought back the misery of the old war wound.

Pinter was close behind when the professor stopped

dead in his tracks, the lantern swinging helplessly by his hip and illuminating the horrible sight at the top of the incline. Ahead of them, the water had seemed to loop round and back.

It was bearing down on them.

Their eyes were wide in horror they watched the torrent advancing down the slope towards them. It was the ultimate trap. Whatever he'd done had triggered the perfect trap. The perfect death.

This was it.

As the two raging waves collided, they'd either be crushed or would drown, their bodies tossed helplessly in the flood.

"There's no way out!" Randle's eyes darted as the water rushed past their ankles. "We're done for!"

His mind raced. Something about this had to make sense. There *had* to be a way out. An access tunnel, a drainage pipe, something.

Pinter took note of the flow of the water, which, rather oddly, seemed to be diverting into a tunnel just out of sight, where it bubbled as it disappeared into a rapidly closing blackness. He grinned.

"Not quite! Look at that crawlspace! I reckon we can fit through. Maybe it's some sort of drain or alternative tunnel?"

The intensity of the water grew and the pressure on their ankles became noticeable. Randle shrugged: "I suppose we have no choice. We either drown or we're buried alive."

"This *must* be a drain. Let's follow it and see where we go. If we stay here we'll die anyway so we may as well find out where this goes. Give me the lantern so that I can take a look!"

Randle handed it over and Pinter got to his stomach, shivering as his shirt was drenched instantly. As he spoke, he spluttered, spitting out the water which now lapped at his lips: "It looks fairly big, and the water keeps moving. Could be our best chance?"

The professor nodded: "It's our only chance."

"I'm glad you agree!"

"You'll be the death of me, Pinter!"

"Just trying to repay the favour, sir," Pinter shouted as he stuck his head and shoulders into the hole and started crawling.

Randle watched for a moment as Pinter and the light disappeared into the tunnel, turning over the scenario in his head. The crash of water bearing down on him prompted a swift decision. He gingerly removed his hat, lay down on his belly, and crawled after his pupil. He was just inside, the Cauldron clasped tightly to his chest, when a huge wave knocked him for six and carried him deep into the bowels of mountain. His hat left his hand and in his panic he almost lost the Cauldron as well, but through the ache of his fingers and the bitter cold he held onto the metal for dear life. He saw the lantern ahead of him crash into a rock. Terror took hold of him as the darkness enveloped him and as he called out for Pinter he found his words muffled by the rushing of water.

Everything went silent and the air disappeared, and though he fought against it, the thick entrails of the water dragged him like a ragdoll beneath the surface, into the inviting blackness.

FOUR

The waterway had opened up into a high-roofed, gentle canal within moments of Pinter and Randle being spat out of the hole in the wall. They'd been right after all – the cavern they now occupied served as a drainage tunnel, and as such water shot out of the entrance they'd used.

The blanket of darkness that had enveloped them was nothing less than opaque, and even when their stinging eyes had adapted to the dim light they couldn't see a thing. All they could tell from the reverberation of their voices was that their tomb was enormous - a fact that was asserted when Pinter reached up to touch the roof of the tunnel and found that he was merely stroking air. Though the gargle of slowly moving water was relaxing, the wintry liquid caused their bodies to shake uncontrollably. Pinter willed his teeth to stop chattering.

If we stay in here for too long, he thought gravely, *we'll sooner freeze to death than drown.*

Randle's voice echoed through the darkness: "Good

thing I kept hold of the Cauldron. Imagine all this effort for nothing!"

"Where are we?"

"Lord knows, but we're not underwater and there's a steady flow. So we're safe for now, I suppose. Or at least...I hope." His tone was grave but it was clear that he was trying his best to be relatively comforting.

"These tunnels must be the result of years of erosion. It's incredible!" Despite himself, Pinter couldn't help but be amazed.

"Or years of construction," Randle added, darkly.

For the first time, they were able to see each other in the darkness as they passed beneath a swathe of glow-worms attached like icicles to the roof of the cavern. The eerie green glow was suitably unusual, and though the light was subdued by their distance from the roof, the illumination was blinding compared to the darkness behind them.

As he turned his body to face Randle, sloshing against the current, Pinter discovered that it was becoming more difficult to fight against the current.

"We're picking up pace."

"You're right." Randle took a look around in the dim light. "We must be nearing an exit tunnel."

"I don't see any light."

"That's what scares me," Randle replied gravely. "How long can you hold your breath?"

"Ten minutes," Pinter tried to joke, but the fear flooded his tone. "Should we try and swim against the current?"

By the time Pinter had managed to get the words out it was too late. Their speed increased dramatically and they were dragged out of the subdued green glow and back into pure darkness.

"Get ready!" Randle spluttered as loud as he could over the din of rushing water. "This could be interesting!"

All too suddenly they were under again, being hauled through an underwater tunnel and rushing against darkness. The plunge had been a surprise, and Pinter was barely able to suck enough air into his lungs before the water had claimed him. His chest was burning, and he knew he had about a minute before he ran out of breath. At the most he could make a minute and a half, but that was really pushing it and he didn't want to test his luck. Not that he had a choice about whether his luck would be tested or not. He could do nothing but let the current pull him and count the seconds in his head, hoping for the best.

He had reached 30 when a dim glimmer of light appeared up ahead. His heart jumped but his lungs screamed as the light got nearer. Panic rushed through him as he counted past 60, and despite his best efforts Pinter couldn't stop the survival instinct as his brain told his body to breathe. He closed his eyes, willing his nose and mouth shut, feeling the roaring pressure of the torrent on his chest.

80 seconds in. He fought his body to keep whatever air he had left shut inside. If he breathed now, he'd be dead.

100 seconds.

Well, he thought morbidly, *at least I've broken my personal best.*

And then, suddenly, at the last imaginable moment, as his mouth opened and he prepared to take a breath, his head broke the surface.

Drinking in the air, he couldn't help but burst out laughing. He was at the base of the waterfall, having shot out from underneath, and he saw the trajectory as Randle emerged, shaken, spluttering, his hat missing, but alive, clutching the Cauldron tightly to his chest with both hands as he tread water painfully.

Pinter's teeth clattered together and his body shook

uncontrollably in the cold, but he didn't give a damn. He was alive. *Only just*, he thought. *But I'm alive.*

"That was a close one," Randle tried to joke, his blue lips quivering too much to allow a smile.

"Too close," Pinter nodded, brushing the wave of sodden hair from out of his eyes. "We got lucky, I guess."

"You certainly did." The voice was new, sardonic. They turned away from each other and looked up in the direction of the camp. Stood at the edge of the water, foot on a rock and arm resting on the knee, was a tall and striking figure in a safari helmet and khaki shorts. His shirt hung open enough for a desert scarf in matching brown to be tucked in comfortably. He was a young man, but with a face that aged him by a decade. Thanks to the thick layer of stubble that covered his jaw, he still held rugged good looks – acne scars all but hidden by the shadow. A fleck of greying brown hair curled out from beneath the safari helmet. After a moment, their only audience member beckoned to his ought-of-sight companions: "Get them out."

Two pairs of meaty fists dragged them from the water, and oddly Randle didn't fight them, instead tightly clutching the Dagda Cauldron. Pinter, on the other hand, tried to shrug them off, landing a futile punch on the chin of the larger of the two. As the thug cracked his knuckles and raised a clenched fist, the safari-helmeted man swiftly interjected: "Not now, Roach. Maybe after."

Roach dropped Pinter abruptly, sending him crashing to the ground. Their leader turned his attention to Randle, removing his safari hat and extending an overly courteous hand: "Dr Randle. My name is Bill Shakespeare. I trust you've heard of me?"

"No." The reply was blunt. Shakespeare seemed to delight in the insult.

"Wonderful. Well, you have now. My friends call me

Bill. You can call me Mr Shakespeare." He paused for effect and took a moment to adjust his shirt, dusting dirt off the knees of his trousers. Apparently satisfied, he smiled politely: "I'd like the Dagda Cauldron now, please."

"The what?"

"Don't be a fool," Shakespeare snorted. "You're holding it in your hand and you know exactly what it is. Lester told me exactly what you were looking for. This was quite the ruse. Even he was fooled for the longest time. It's a shame really...if only you hadn't have been so careless with who you trusted."

Randle shot Pinter a look.

"Lester? He didn't have a clue what he was talking about. This was an expedition to investigate Neolithic settlements." Randle's bluff was a poor one. Pinter had to stop his eyes from rolling as Randle realised he still held the Cauldron in his hand.

"Where is Lester?" The question seemed more out of civility and ignored Randle's ploy completely. By the tone in his voice, it was clear that Shakespeare didn't really care about their treacherous companion at all.

"Sorry Bill," Pinter replied. "He kicked the proverbial bucket."

"And who," Shakespeare sneered, "are you, old chap?"

"Rupert Pinter. But you can call me a thorn in your side if you want."

"Pinter? How quaint." Shakespeare ignored the rest of the remark, though he seemed vaguely amused by the idea of someone standing up to him. Rupert nodded back to the cave entrance behind the waterfall:

"What's left of Lester is in there. Maybe you should go and get him...with him being such a good chum of yours."

"I think I'll leave him be. He was always too greedy for his own good. A shame. He was paid well."

"He never got to use it," Randle spat. "And who exactly are *you* working for?"

Shakespeare pulled out a Luger in reply, cocking it as he did so. "Never you mind, old man. Now...hand it over and I may spare you like I did the rest of this pathetic *expedition* of yours."

Randle sighed and reluctantly handed the Cauldron over.

"Good man," Shakespeare grinned, before turning to Pinter: "Now be a nice chap and follow my men down the mountain, would you?" He turned then to Roach, a sneer in his voice: "Kill him when you reach the bottom. Throw his body in the river. We can't have any evidence of this. Not like that mess you made of Tirey. Kill the boy first. I'd like to have a short chat with old Geoffrey here in the mean time."

Randle's eyes filled with pain, but the rest of him simply shrugged. "Tirey taught me a few words to live by, young man. It's a Chinese proverb. 'If you must play, decide on three things at the start: the rules of the game, the stakes, and the quitting time.' Rather poignant, don't you think? Cheerio, Rupert. I'll give your father your regards when I see him."

Oddly, the professor's eyes motioned to his student's gun-belt. Pinter shot Randle a knowing look. Though sodden and useless, his Mark IV Webley revolver hung loosely inside his holster. As the thugs dragged him up, he reached for it.

By the time they had dragged him out of Shakespeare's line of sight it was too late for them. In one fluid motion, Pinter brought up the butt of the gun, swung a nose cracking arc across the skulls of both men, and had broken into a run before they even knew what, or who, had hit them.

FIVE

By the time Roach had managed to shake the stars from his eyes, wipe the blood from his re-broken nose and grab Lawrence, the slightly shorter, slightly leaner thug, Pinter had already made it half-way down the mountain path and was out of sight, disappearing beneath the brow of the hill.

Roach was a large man. He was certainly more muscle than brain, which led in no small part to his dishonourable discharge from the forces, and his thick set frame was more appropriate for brute force than pursuit. As such, he grimaced at the thought of a prolonged chase and reluctantly took off after the considerably smaller, speedier Pinter. Lawrence, also an ex-Army type but suspended for the simple reason that he didn't know how to disagree with Roach, was on the other hand well aware that he wasn't qualified for the task at hand. He immediately turned on his heel and jogged up the path to re-join Shakespeare.

Their employer was now locked in a bitter skirmish with the old man, who wrestled viciously for ownership of the

Dagda Cauldron. Shakespeare was surprised at the strength of the old man, but in the end, all it really took was a hearty shove from Lawrence to swing the odds in their favour and send Randle toppling backwards into the icy splash-pool. The Cauldron was left firmly gripped in Shakespeare's hands, and Bill allowed himself an amused laugh at the sight of Randle spluttering and shivering in the water, before he turned on his heel and vanished out of sight, following the trail in the opposite direction to the route Pinter and Roach had taken.

Aware that their attackers had now withdrawn, Randle's students crept slowly from their tents, their faces white with terror. Seeing their tutor treading water, they immediately and wordlessly pulled him out.

Nobody said a thing. The fear had gripped them too tightly for idle chit-chat. Randle looked around his flock, counting heads. Lester was naturally going to be absent, but there was one more person missing from the group.

His blood ran cold.

Downstream, Pinter seemed to have the upper-hand, taking the high road that rested on a bank above the river. Roach was close behind now, running on the low road that ran parallel, but Pinter was running out of steam and the thug seemed to be looking for any ample opportunity to scramble up the bank after him without losing too much ground and cut the foot chase short.

There was only so much longer this could go on for, and Pinter knew full well that in a few minutes it would effectively be game over. He wasn't a hugely athletic fellow, and though the early morning walks had done wonders for his lung capacity, the month he'd spent kneeling in a trench brushing mud had ruined his aerobic stamina.

That fact he'd been half drowned a few minutes earlier

did little to help the situation, of course.

His legs felt like they were about to fall off, but he kept going anyway, pure adrenaline driving him forwards.

Running for your life does wonders for your performance in sport, he thought.

The path was uneven, and all it took was a small rock, embedded in centuries of soil and noticeable only if you were actively looking for it, to trip him over and send him sprawling clumsily to the ground. Pinter lost his footing completely as he struck the stone and in the momentum of the run he tumbled headfirst down the bank, colliding painfully with Roach as he did so.

They fought with the fall and with each other as Roach posed to tackle the younger man and, to his surprise, found himself knocked off his feet. They grappled without flair or grace, trying where they could to land weak punches as they rolled off the path and onto the edge of the river with an agonising thud.

Pinter realised too late that they were heading for the fall and shrugged the thug off, reaching desperately for something to grab on to as a brake.

There was no such luck.

Strands of dew-stained grass came away in his hands and his breath leapt from his lungs as they plunged into the icy water.

Though Roach went for him again, both men resigned to exhausted, frosty defeat as their attacks were rendered hopeless, instead letting the flow of the river take them as the velocity increased inexplicably. Within moments, they reached a narrowing – tight rocks hemming them in on either side and an inky blackness awaiting them beyond. The river seemed to drop into nothingness.

As his head tentatively broke the surface Pinter managed to splutter "Not again..." before sucking in a deep breath.

The two of them caught each other's eyes, sharing a look moments before they pitched downwards and into the murky gloom.

**

When he remerged, bloodied from a battering by rocks and the riverbed as he was flung like a spoilt child's plaything in the throes of the torrent, Pinter noticed with stinging eyes that Roach was nowhere to be seen. He was practically at the bottom of the mountain now, having rolled to a stop when the river opened wide and the speed slowed to that of a stream. He guessed he must've rolled the rest of the way down, gently prodded onwards by the water as it flowed out of the valley.

As he dragged himself out of the water, stumbling with punch-drunk grace, he noticed a small arched bridge above him.

The road.

Which meant he was near the trucks that they had travelled to the expedition from Oxford in.

It meant he was closer to safety. For the moment.

It also meant that he'd travelled almost a mile. Clutching his head, he felt for cuts or grazes, but didn't get a chance to thoroughly inspect the damage as all at once the heavy figure of Roach bounced and splashed into view.

The sound of an aging vehicle echoed from further up the road. Quickly, and as quietly as he could, Pinter hid himself behind the bridge and out of sight.

Dazed, alarmed, and not for the first time extremely confused, Roach rubbed his freshly destroyed nose as the passenger door of the waiting Bedford truck swung open. He pulled himself to his feet, and scratched his head as he took a look around. The boy was nowhere to be seen. It seemed impossible that he hadn't noticed Pinter's corpse being flung past him as they rushed downstream. Regardless, Roach took some solace in the idea that the river had killed the boy, rubbing his nose again in surprise. Perhaps the cold had numbed the pain, but it was as though he couldn't feel it at all.

With great effort he hopped over the fence by the road climbed into the waiting flat-bed truck and slammed the door as the truck rattled away. Pinter waited until they were but a mere speck on the horizon before emerging from his hiding place and collapsing on the grass beside the river.

He did a self assessment of his injuries. Nothing was seriously damaged, but he'd badly bruised his knees and his nose bled. He held his head in his hands for a moment.

The sun finally emerged and Rupert Pinter allowed himself a moment to soak up the limited winter heat into his bruised body. Though the morning was frosty, the air was like a warm blanket on his skin after the sub-zero temperature of the river. He was desperate for a hot bath, a cup of tea and a good night's sleep, but he knew that would be a long time coming. First a trek back up the mountain to find Randle, then a journey back to Oxford and an inevitable dressing down from the university.

He hadn't realised yet, but the coppery taste of blood filled his taste-buds. He cringed in disgust and spat out a mouthful, discerning that his skirmish with Roach had left him with a loose tooth.

And a bruised ego.

Something for another day, he shrugged.

The most curious element of the whole ordeal was this Shakespeare fellow. He had no idea who he was, no idea where he'd come from, and no idea where he'd found the money to grease Lester's pockets, but he could tell that there was something sinister about this business. It struck him that maybe they'd narrowly escaped the same fate as Tirey...and for the same reason. It was simply a case of waiting now. Something was bound to turn up eventually – it normally did.

Grudgingly, knowing full well that rising to his feet would simply bring more suffering, Pinter dragged himself from the ground. He adjusted his drenched clothes, pulling his sodden work shirt from his skin. His cap was resting against a rock in the middle of the river, so he leant over and reached for it, shaking out as much of the damp as he could before mashing it onto his skull. He smoothed the brim, and then started on the long path back to Randle, his shoes squelching uncomfortably as he did so.

SIX

Oxford University
TWO WEEKS LATER

It was entertaining watching the white vein throbbing against crimson skin as the sanity of the Dean of Oxford University slowly waned. Pinter felt a childish urge to laugh as the wild-eyed Professor Alexander Harding-Rosenthal ranted and raved without much semblance of clarity. Beside him, Dr James McCalvin, the 'good-cop' to Harding-Rosenthal's bad, sat twiddling his thumbs and twitching occasionally as the volume of his superior shattered his ear drums.

"And furthermore..."

It had continued for the best part of an hour when Harding-Rosenthal, finally drained of all colour but scarlet, collapsed back into the high backed leather chair and allowed McCalvin to speak. The calm, relaxed tone was a breath of fresh air:

"We're not trying to pin the blame on you in the slightest, Rupert. It was an unforeseen, impossible circumstance that you just happened to be part of. You have to realise, however, that this whole affair has put the university in a very difficult position."

"Which I do, believe me, but I don't see why I'm being made into a villain in all this," Pinter protested. "I've done nothing wrong."

"Villain isn't the word we'd use, Rupert," McCalvin cut in. "Rather...well, I suppose the best term to use would be problem child."

"I resent that."

"I have no doubt. Don't feel that we're trying to victimise you, Mr Pinter, we're simply trying to deconstruct the glaring flaws in the expedition to Wales."

"This is absurd."

"There is no record of this 'Shakespeare' and a student died, Pinter! So you'll understand why we've ended Dr Randle's tenure."

Pinter sat back and crossed his arms sullenly: "You fired him?"

"A necessary evil," McCalvin grimaced. "He was a good teacher. A great teacher, one of our best. But our establishment can't be seen to support this."

"And what about me? Are you getting rid of me too?" Pinter rubbed his still sore cheek, the red bruise slowly starting to fade after a week of ice-packs.

"No, no. You were caught in the crossfire. We'd seriously recommend that you re-evaluate your position in this university, Rupert. Randle is an old family friend of yours, we're well aware of that. We can appreciate the relationship he had with your father and his attitudes towards you as a result. But you need to choose your friends more carefully from now on. Keep your head down, or we may have to expel you from this establishment. Stay away from Geoffrey Randle, Mr Pinter. The man is trouble. Even your father knew that."

"My father trusted Geoffrey Randle with his life."

"And look where it left him," Harding-Rosenthal murmured. "Lost without trace in China, presumed dead because he was chasing after some sort of childish dream."

The words were biting, brutal, and for a moment Pinter couldn't believe he'd just heard them. He fought back tears as they began to well in his eyes, and bit his tongue rather than say something he might regret.

"Your father was a good man, Rupert. But not infallible. And neither are you, so I seriously suggest that you collect the necessary papers on your way out from Miss Hues, my secretary, and start doing some work for your degree, rather than these 'extra-curricular activities'. Your father disapproved of your choice of course, and by God, he'd disapprove of your actions. You should be ashamed of yourself."

"With all due respect," Pinter said, his tone almost menacing as he chose his words extremely carefully: "I don't think you knew my father at all, Doctor Harding-Rosenthal. Will that be all?"

Pinter closed the panelled oak door behind him gently and breathed a deep sigh that was a mixture of relief, frustration, and rage. He could hardly believe the treatment of Randle. As for his father...

Fools, he thought, fury bubbling through his veins. *Miserable fools.*

He stuffed the papers he'd collected from the secretary into his pocket and grabbed his coat from a hook beside the door. He hadn't noticed Lana Marlowe step up beside him until he bumped into her.

"You look a little worse for wear."

Too weary to be startled, he managed a smile: "Had a wonderful chat with Harding-Rosenthal and McCalvin. Well," he shrugged. "With McCalvin anyway. Harding-Rosenthal seemed more interested in driving the knife as deep as he could about my father."

"Harding-Rosenthal could talk for England if he wanted to."

"Do you mean shout?"

Lana giggled: "I do, yes."

He took her books and they started through the impressive décor of the corridors, out into the gardens below. As they emerged into the fresh air Pinter considered for a moment that his day was looking up. Despite still aching from the escapade a couple of weeks earlier he was in the company of the most-beautiful red-head he'd ever seen.

They strolled gently to a free patch of grass and Pinter collapsed onto the soft ground, the sun warming his clothes. He could hardly believe it was early February. The crisp morning air had paved way to a gorgeous afternoon – the sort of afternoon where the biting cold was fighting a losing battle with an optimistic sun. Lana lay down beside him, resting her head on his shoulder blade. For a moment they said nothing, watching as students hurried across the courtyard to their lectures. Others were sat around the grounds, reading hefty tomes on the benches or eating sandwiches under the canopies of trees dotted around them. It was just another Monday morning, just another start to just another semester. Eventually Lana took his hand and hitched herself onto her elbow so that she could look at him:

"You do have to be more careful, though, Roop."

"I'm careful enough."

"I just don't want to see your academic career cut short. You worked hard enough to get here in the first place."

"Harding-Rosenthal doesn't seem to think so. He's convinced I'm here on my father's merits rather than my own. And I *am* being careful."

"Are you?"

She stroked his hair playfully. When he talked about his father, Rupert tended to close off. She didn't like it, but what else could she expect? The pair had never truly seen eye to eye before Pinter Senior's death, and she knew that it was one of the things Rupert regretted, even if he didn't want to say as much.

Similarly, he pushed himself up onto his elbow to look at her and caught genuine concern. Giving her a cheeky half-smile, he tried to be reassuring: "Trust me. It'll be fine."

"Ok. Don't pay any heed to Harding-Rosenthal. He's not the sort of person you should be losing sleep over." She reached into her bag and pulled out an envelope. "I want you to have this, by the way."

Pinter opened it up and pulled out an invitation. Lana explained before he could read it: "Its black tie. Aboard my father's company zeppelin on Saturday night. Thought you might be interested. Some sort of artifact on display. A royal flush, as my father puts it."

"The Sword of Nuada?" Pinter read aloud. "Sounds vaguely Celtic to me. What is it?"

"I'm not sure. You'd have to ask my father that – he's become obsessed with the damn thing. But this beats his obsession with aero-dynamism. I hoped that once the Ministry of Defence funded the zeppelin he was obsessing over then he'd finally stop talking about the damn thing. He did, but replaced it with this, unfortunately. It should be a fun night though. Will you come?"

Pinter smiled: "Why not? I'd love to."

"Good." She flushed an embarrassed red in the space of a few short moments. "Dress well. I imagine you'd look good in a tuxedo."

"I look forward to it."

She winked and got up, scooping her books into her arms. "I have to go. I'll see you on Saturday, then?"

He nodded, smiling. "Wouldn't miss it for the world."

She grinned, and Pinter watched as she departed, her skirt carried in the wind and her red hair flowing. It was amazing how Lana could so swiftly change his mood. All thoughts of his father had gone, and he wasn't even particularly bothered about the dressing down he'd had from the University either. The day really was looking up, after all.

Studying the invite once more, Pinter felt a creeping suspicion of the Celtic artifact on display. It all seemed a bit too unlikely to be a coincidence. Perhaps Randle and Tirey knew something he didn't? And maybe even his father was in on it? They had all moved in the same circles in Oxford, all been quite good friends. They'd all fought in the trenches together. Randle had even practically adopted him when his father died.

"What have you gotten me into now, Randle?" He wondered aloud. "What on earth have you gotten me into?"

There was cautious, and there was the sort of cautious that Pinter knew all too well. It was the sort that bordered on reckless. A dangerous sort of caution.

SEVEN

A cold wind caught the neckline of Bill Shakespeare and he drew his collar up under his chin as he paced steadily along the winding, weed-bitten path that led through the desolate graveyard of Liverpool Cathedral. As he followed the trail up the gentle incline, past crumbling tombs that were decorated with thick entrails of unyielding moss, he nodded in morbid acknowledgement to a clergyman, also wrapped up against the northern chill and laying a wreath on a gravestone that glistened with frost. Father Dadd nodded back, but didn't smile, instead regarding Shakespeare with a look of concerned interest. It was the sort of look that implied Shakespeare was exactly the sort of man the church was guarded from.

It was depressingly February. Shakespeare rued the fact that he was this far north. He was definitely a Southerner, and the cold disagreed with him considerably. Even the thick woolen scarf he sported over his knee-length black trench-coat did little to ward off the biting teeth of the mid-winter breeze. At once he wished he were abroad, as he normally was this time of year, sipping sangria on the coast of Spain or mint tea in the souks of Arabia. 1932 had proved to be a damned bad year for weather so far, and he could only hope that it would improve. Having to stay bound to the United Kingdom and its awful weather was more of a chore than he'd imagined.

Still, Shakespeare considered, *it is a means to an end and a large cheque at the finish-line.*

He pushed against the heavy doors of the church and felt the drop in temperature immediately. It was as if he were stepping into a freezer in the Arctic. His teeth clattered together violently, only stopping when he willed them to stop and when the shaking of his hands became a distraction as he reluctantly removed the thick leather gloves preventing his fingers from dropping off.

The cathedral was enormous, appearing to stretch for miles into the murky distance. The stained glass windows cast foreboding shadows with the thin winter light that crept through, and while their colours seemed to dance on the floor, the church itself was mostly cloaked in darkness. The flickering of candles that lined the row of pews did little to help the visibility, but he expected that that was exactly what the man he was here to meet was hoping for. As he walked deeper into the nucleus of the building, the soft tones of a choir singing Repton's *Dear Lord and Father of Mankind* echoed into every nook and cranny of the cathedral. The song had a despondent edge to it, the voices of the choirboys floating towards him.

Sat in a wooden pew further down the church was a suited figure who seemed impervious to the lack of heat. He sat facing the font, head still and clean-cut hair oiled and frozen in place.

There was something that wasn't right about all this. A

sinister feeling ran through his blood. Shakespeare hated churches. They gave him the creeps. There was something about religion he didn't like. Perhaps it was the divine that scared him, or the uncertainty. He couldn't be sure.

"You know full well that I don't like these places." He kept his voice to a low whisper as he addressed his contact, sliding onto a pew behind and bowing his head as if immersed in prayer.

"This is the most inconspicuous place for us to meet. And your lack of specific faith is why we hired you, Mr Shakespeare."

"That's comforting." Shakespeare wasn't sure whether to be pleased or not about their accurate perception of his beliefs. He liked to assume he had an open mind.

"We like to think so."

"You wanted to see me?"

"You did well in Wales."

This is the reason they called me here? Shakespeare was incandescent with rage. He hadn't wasted almost an entire day's travel on an uncomfortable second-class train seat for hollow congratulations. Furrowing his brow, but swallowing the bulk of his anger, he said bluntly: "I didn't come for praise. Is this important?"

A gust of wind whipped through the church, whistling through the rafters.

"Tomorrow night," the suited man replied after a time, "The Sword of Nuada is within our grasp at last. You failed us on the Orient Express the first time you attempted to retrieve it. Do not fail again, or we may be required to retire you of your services. This would not be a suitable arrangement for us and I would imagine that it would be even less so for you."

"Is that some sort of threat?"

"Let us hope that we do not find out."

As the stinging sense of discomfort swept through him, Shakespeare cast his mind back to Turkey, some months earlier. How close he had been then...had Theodore Marlowe not sent the Sword ahead. It had been a nasty misfortune that having stopped the train in the dead of night just outside Istanbul with an army of heavily armed Turks at his side, a turbaned Shakespeare had opened the supply carriage running at the back of the train to discover a selection of rugs and an assortment of bemused animals. It had been an unmitigated disaster that had left Shakespeare with a large amount of egg on his face. An opportunity to catch up with Marlowe would be one he certainly wouldn't want to miss. He remembered Marlowe distinctly from society dinners at the Conservative Club. A bear of a man, with an awful laugh that invaded every conversation in the room. You could tell if Marlowe was in attendance if a good joke was told and the laughter was deafening. The sheer arrogance of the man amused him further – a failed diplomat that had made a career out of warmongering. The British way, perhaps, but the lines of pacifism were clearly defined, and Marlowe seemed to jump in and out of either school of thought whenever he felt appropriate. *The first rule of business*, thought Shakespeare, *is to decide exactly which business you're in.*

"There is one problem." The grave tone of the suited man was deathly even in the dark recesses of the church.

"There always is," Shakespeare mused, expecting nothing less. "Go on?"

"It will be on display at a private party."

"Where?"

"Aboard his zeppelin."

A grin traced Shakespeare's expression: "I'd imagine that it will be quite the party. I assume you didn't get me an invitation?"

"We hired you to take care of those things yourself."

"I thought so. It sounds like it could be quite difficult." He paused, scratching his chin in anticipation: "It sounds like fun."

EIGHT

Pinter took a firm grip on the iron railing of the thin boarding platform and gazed up at the massive blimp that hung precariously in the sky above him. It shimmered with a gunmetal silver glow, floating like a bullet that sat perpetually in flight. The *Carthaginian Storm* was a custom construction, funded by Marlowe Industries, and thanks, in part, to a generous donation by the government for 'services to historical artifact acquisition'. Those in the higher echelons of government, however, had no doubt that should the situation of the Empire overseas worsen, or lead dreadfully to another war, the *Carthaginian* would be the first flight to leave London, albeit equipped for a much less noble purpose. It stood as a monument to the British Empire itself – grand and flamboyant, and not particularly necessary.

In that sense, the *Carthaginian Storm* was to Britain what the *Hindenburg* was to Germany, though Marlowe was known to boast of the prowess of British Engineering:

using less dangerous gasses than hydrogen to significantly reduce the danger of air travel.

"Those bloody Jerries," Marlowe often boasted, "will find themselves in hot water rather than hot air sooner or later!"

His words were marked with a poignant edge. Two years earlier had seen the crash of the *R101*, the flagship of the Imperial Airship Scheme. Marlowe had been involved with the construction, and had left the project after a falling out with a technician about the safety of the craft. The *Carthaginian* dwarfed the *R101* in both scope and scale, but with a greater degree of safety – an insistence of Marlowe from the first day of construction.

Stepping into the lavishly decorated undercarriage, Pinter couldn't help but smile at the sheer number of famous and infamous faces around him. The place was a venerable rogues gallery. He adjusted his bow-tie and smoothed the lapels of his tuxedo before making his way up a winding, red-carpeted stairway and into the ballroom of the airship.

Having already seen the size of the zeppelin from his approach to the airfield, it shouldn't have surprised Pinter that the chamber was enormous, but nevertheless he held back a gasp in awe of the construction. The sheer volume of the airship was staggering. It the perfect venue for such an occasion. He could only wonder at the cost of the steel beast. The walls of the ballroom, which stretched high above them, were lined with red curtains. Bunting draped the wall, and directly behind the main stage was a colossal Union Flag that hung majestically from the ceiling. A big-band was in full swing, accompanying the laughter and conversation that wafted from the dance-floor to the rafters.

Ahead of him, in a glass box, sealed and guarded by security guards that looked more like gorillas in dinner jackets, was the Sword of Nuada.

For a moment he stood close to the exhibit, entranced by its simple beauty. It had no extravagant gold lining or encrusted diamonds that one may expect from an object of such prominence, instead appearing as just an average sword. Oddly, the Sword hadn't aged in the slightest, gleaming as though new. It was as though it had been cast that very morning, and the most extraordinary element of the artifact was the complete lack of any sort of age marks. It led Pinter to question how on Earth they'd managed to date the thing.

A question for Mr Marlowe later on this evening, he considered. *Perhaps after I've had a few whiskeys to calm my nerves.*

Looking closer, Pinter saw a variety of Celtic symbols engraved on the hilt, and for a moment considered tracing his finger across the glass in their swirling, carefree shapes. There was something beautifully haunting about Celtic symbology, one that seemed to ooze romance. To Pinter, at least. He'd spent most of the first semester of his linguistics course dedicated to learning more about the languages they weren't taught. Latin was standard – all public schoolboys knew their Latin, and his school in Worcestershire had made perfectly sure that Pinter had left with a very capable application of the language. Ancient Greek was trickier, if only for the lack of translation resources and Ancient Latin was a variation of sorts on the modern. It was the symbology and linguistic intricacies of ancient cultures that fascinated Pinter. His tutors were suitably unimpressed.

The sudden jolt of the mooring cables detaching and the airship taking flight, combined with the impact of a strong palm colliding with his shoulder, almost knocked him over. As the other occupants of the ballroom laughed with nervous embarrassment, Pinter spun around and into a cloud of thick cigar smoke, desperately holding in the severe coughing fit that threatened to envelope him.

"Quite something, huh?" The broad shouldered, impeccably dressed, red-faced, mustachioed American who stood before him chewed on a fat Havana cigar as he spoke in a sprawling Southern drawl: "Don't you think?"

"Certainly. Quite the accomplishment for Mr Marlowe."

"Sure is." A large fist opened to an outstretched palm: "Raymond Ellroy. Ellroy Oil." Ellroy struck Pinter as being the kind of man that had come from family money, not uncommon where oil was concerned. He had the belly to prove it, though he successfully managed to hide his gut beneath the cummerbund of his white tuxedo. He was completely bald, but had thick, bushy eyebrows that matched his moustache in size, as if to compensate the lack of hair on his head. Oddly, the eyebrows seemed to connect with the thick, round spectacles that perched about a large, red-nose. For a moment, Pinter imagined him with a white Stetson on – an image which seemed to suit him quite well. Perhaps Ellroy would indeed manage to adhere to the stereotypical picture of the oil baron.

"Rupert Pinter. There's no company name for me, I'm afraid. I'm a student at Oxford University. Lana Marlowe's guest for this evening."

"The daughter's boyfriend, huh?" Ellroy grinned with a childish mischief that didn't seem to suit an American Oil Executive. His blood-shot eyes twinkled with delight.

"Not quite."

"Not yet, huh?" He winked. "Good man."

"So how do you know Mr Marlowe, Mr Ellroy?"

"Ray. Please. This is my night off. A drink?" He nodded to a waiter, who obediently hurried over. "Two scotch on the rocks. That alright with you, Rupert?"

Pinter shrugged. "Don't see why not, I suppose. The bar

is free, isn't it?"

The heavy palm crushed his shoulder again, "It is for us, but I like the way you think."

The drinks arrived almost instantly and the scotch in Ellroy's glass vanished into his portly stomach before Pinter had even wrapped a hand around his own tumbler. Ellroy could certainly drink. Coughing slightly on the fumes from his cigar, Ellroy rapped his chest and finally answered the earlier question: "I met Theo at a conference a few years back. Decent guy," he motioned around the room: "but head in the clouds. We provide the oil for his airship and other projects. In return, he runs materials back and forth across the pond for us."

"Quite a lucrative deal."

"I'd say so, but I'm not here for business. And I'd say neither were you." His eyes moved across to a doorway, where Lana had appeared, dressed in a swirling black number that fitted in all the right places. Pinter felt his jaw drop and with her usual perfect timing Lana saw him. She grinned with pleasure and made her way over. Ellroy smiled and departed, nodding knowingly, as Lana reached them: "You made it then, Rupert?"

"It seems so. Lana, you look..." he could hardly speak.

"I try."

"You definitely succeed."

The band struck up Gershwin's *The Man I Love* and Lana's eyes lit up. "I love this song."

Before he could react, Pinter was being dragged headfirst onto the dance-floor. Lana pulled him close and placed his hand on her hip. He could smell the coconut scent of her dark red hair as her cheek rested against his. He wasn't a dancer by any means but a determination to impress flooded into his two left feet and he struggled valiantly to keep in time. Lana smiled to herself with every mis-step that he made, apparently impressed that she'd finally discovered something about Pinter that could taint his usually unwavering confidence. She considered that slow-dancing wasn't a particularly hard art to master. It simply had to be done right.

She'd decided well ahead of time, though, that she was going to forgive him this indiscretion.

"Calm down, Roop. You're not out to impress anyone here but me."

"That's what I'm trying to do," he whispered back. "Can't you tell?"

"You're trying too hard."

"I know, but I thought that you of all people would appreciate it," he winked, trying to hide his embarrassment at how useless he was turning out to be at slow dancing. "Maybe I should've learnt to dance before I came?"

"Just relax and dance with me," she murmured, before resting her head on his shoulder and falling silent. They swayed in time to the music and Pinter felt butterflies in his chest trying to escape. She held him close, and her body warmed him. He couldn't help but smile.

I'm dancing with a knockout, he thought.

All the chaps at the Daggers Club couldn't help but loathe Pinter for his relationship with Lana Marlowe. That Pinter had yet to make a move was the object of plenty of derision. *If only they could see me now*, Pinter grinned. *They'd be having kittens.*

It was only after the music came to an end that Pinter realised, to his abject horror, they were the only ones dancing. His cheeks flushed as a generous applause from impressed guests saw them off the dance-floor. The band struck up a jazzy number to allow the reception to comfortably mingle. Pinter felt his shoulder shudder again as the thin palm of Theodore Marlowe clasped him.

"So, you're Rupert Pinter then? I say, you're the spit of your father! I only met him once or twice but it's as though he's standing before me now!"

"Yes, sir!" Pinter took his outstretched palm and shook it. "Thank you for the invitation."

"More than welcome, my boy. My daughter told me you needed it. Nasty business in Wales. Nasty country, in fact."

Marlowe seemed fairly jovial, which wasn't surprising. He had a thick mop of salt and pepper hair and stood quite tall, at least a shoulder above Pinter. If he was any shorter, perhaps he could have been considered slightly overweight, but the balance of his height and width gave him instead an imposing figure.

Pinter noticed, as the head of Marlowe Industries looked him up and down, that Lana had his eyes, though Theodore's were more weathered, bearing a pained look.

"From a certain perspective I can agree, yes."

"Very diplomatic. You know, if you learnt to dance properly you'd be quite good. Lana doesn't seem to mind, though," he winked. "Perhaps we can talk after. I saw the way you were admiring the Sword. We could discuss more of the history? I've no doubt at all that an observant fellow such as yourself is wondering how we can be certain that it's the real deal, particularly as it looks brand new...and I had wondered the same thing myself when we opened the burial mound in Constantinople..." he laughed to himself and slapped his forehead. "But I digress. I shall come and find you after the speech, and we can discuss these matters over a scotch."

"I'd like that very much, sir." Pinter held out his hand once again. Marlowe took it and shook it firmly.

"So would I. See you after my big moment then, Rupert." He grinned and then turned to Lana as she appeared from across the room, a pair of glasses in her hands: "My dear, you look wonderful. The image of your mother. She would no doubt be even more proud than I am this evening. Keep this young man company for a moment, and don't let him run off. He and I have important historical matters to discuss, and they've waited long enough." He smiled broadly and headed off towards the stage.

"He likes you," said Lana, handing Pinter a glass of champagne. "He really likes you."

"How can you tell?"

"He used your first name."

Pinter smiled and shrugged before taking her hand and disappearing into the crowd as Marlowe took the stage.

"Good evening!" He announced: "Thank you for joining us. Tonight, I'd like to talk about a fantastic piece of history."

NINE

There was a bated silence as Marlowe commanded the stage. As he loudly cleared his throat, Pinter got the distinct impression that Theodore Marlowe had done this before.

"We have before us evidence of the scraps of truth in myth. An impossible acquisition that logic dictates should not exist. But then if that were a fact of life, then I would not be here myself." He paused for laughter, drinking in the moment. Those who knew of Marlowe's past, which happened to be everyone except Pinter, were reminded of his favourite anecdote of a birth that almost wasn't.

He continued: "What we have before us is the Sword of Nuada. Weapon of legend, lost in the bloodshed of war, transported from the realm of the Celts to the bloody North, and eventually through the centuries winding its way to Turkey, where in the dying throes of the Ottoman Empire it became a symbol of divine power. This is an object drenched in life and death, but let me tell you more of the supposed history rather than the facts. You'll have to forgive me, Reverend Dawkins," he nodded to the archbishop, who smiled and raised a glass in return, "but skeptics like myself see this as significant only as evidence for archaeology of Early Britain. If we were to believe, however, perhaps that there were some grounding to the fanciful stories of Early Celtic mythology, then the Sword of Nuada features heavily in the 'Four Treasures' Myth, the basic gist of which is a collection of four prominent objects of Irish lore. If this sword truly was held by the god-king Nuada himself, we would behold here, in a sense, a relic of the Otherworld and a link to a world beyond our own."

The speech continued in a similar vein, but Pinter had already felt his blood run cold.

It can't be.

His hand gripped Lana's tightly and she turned to look at him with a mixture of anger and fear flashing across her grey eyes. "What's wrong?"

"I've got a nasty feeling, that's all."

"Oh, hush," she murmured, rolling her eyes. "We're perfectly safe up here."

"Being 'up here' is what scares me," he hissed.

The mention of the four treasures had already turned Pinter white and sent him back to the caverns in Wales. He had held the Dagda Cauldron in his own hands, been eyewitness to another piece of the puzzle, and watched helplessly as it was snatched away from them before they'd even had a chance to explore its intricacies. Surely it was only a matter of time before someone came for the Sword?

This is why background reading is important, he said to himself. *I should have known this before I even got on the bloody blimp.*

He shook the fears away as base paranoia. This seemed too untrue to be a coincidence but for all he knew, Tirey was simply spurred on in his quest for the Cauldron by news of Marlowe's expedition in Turkey. Perhaps it was a rivalry of sorts. The men were, after all, occupying the same social circles. Perhaps the shrewd nature of financial backing was to blame here and not much else.

Pinter doubted it. Something didn't sit well at with the whole business. Had Marlowe been involved in Tirey's death?

Marlowe by now was rounding up his speech: "...and so I'd like to ask you all to raise your glasses in a toast to such an important piece of history and to its position of pride and joy, at the forefront of the newly installed Celtic Pre-History section in the Chapman Andrews Hall of the National History Museum in New York. Here is to a long life of the Sword of Nuada, and the generations to come that will be able to marvel at such an incredible piece."

There was a rapturous applause. Those who were sat stood, and those who were already standing clapped louder in appreciation. Marlowe had certainly picked a bunch that would provide a decent level of ovation. The clapping died off gradually as Marlowe shook hands with some of the men who stood near him on the stage, before departing from the podium and plunging into the crowd. His audience immediately moved forward, eager to shake his hand.

After the murmuring of approval at the speech had begun, one pair of hands continued to clap obnoxiously. A hushed silence fell almost immediately and attention turned to a younger man, perhaps a few years older than Pinter, who stepped confidently through the crowd. In his khaki he stood out amongst the tuxedoed guests and Pinter cursed himself for not having seen him sooner.

Bill Shakespeare sipped at a glass of champagne as the room fell completely silent and he was able to cease clapping, expecting fizzy wine but emerging surprised:

"This is actually quite good. Expensive stuff. You throw quite the soiree, Marlowe. I'm very impressed. Very impressed indeed."

"Who the hell are you?" Lana's father was apoplectic.

"My name is Bill Shakespeare. No matter, though," he drew his Luger and elicited a scream from a woman nearby, who nearly fainted. "I would very much like for you all to stand still while I take the Sword. If everyone behaves, I may let you all live. I'm sure you can all understand the position you're in, so I hope no-one here will try to be a hero. My men are all over this airship and I can send it crashing to the ground within moments."

As Shakespeare moved towards the glass display case, Pinter slipped out of sight, a plan formulating in his head. How had he not seen this coming? All the signs were there!

The one thing he could take from this nightmare was that he was right. There was definitely something afoot. Perhaps this was a long standing plan, but all the pieces were falling into place at the right time?

It didn't matter for now. What did matter was staying out of sight until he had a clearer idea of exactly what to do. His eyes traced the walls – service entrances, maintenance tunnels, anything. How was Shakespeare planning on getting out?

There were sub-machinegun toting men all over the place – obviously friends of Shakespeare. It would explain why the dinner-jacketed thugs Marlowe had hired for protection weren't doing anything. He counted seven of Shakespeare's comrades, but added an extra two for good measure. He simply couldn't know how many were hidden out of sight.

He couldn't take them all on either. It would be ridiculous and he would have his backside handed to him instantly. They had machine-guns and he'd gone and left his revolver at home, assuming he wouldn't need it.

You bloody idiot, Pinter cursed himself silently. *Next time, trust your instincts.*

The best course of action for now, it seemed, was to stay hidden.

Concealed by the crowd, he grabbed Lana and they quickly slipped under the buffet table and out of sight, veiled by the tablecloth.

"Don't say a word," he hissed, and she nodded, more out of fear than anything else.

The glass case exploded and Shakespeare gently lifted the Sword from its stand and into his arms, where he wrapped it in cloth. As he lifted it, a piece of parchment fell from the hilt, and he leant to pick it up, raising his eyebrows in surprise. No-one moved, too entranced by the combination of confident swagger and careful preservation on display. Another man, dressed in black and wielding a Suomi sub-machine gun appeared from the wings and was handed the Sword. Pinter recognised him immediately as the tank of a man he'd brawled with on the mountain – the man Shakespeare had called Roach. The other man was there too, Lawrence, lurking in the wings, but looking equally as nasty with a machine gun.

As quickly as he had appeared, Roach was gone, and with a gunslinger's swagger Shakespeare headed for the door. "I must say, you were all very good."

A crackling voice came over the loudspeaker, echoing through the now silent room: "We're in the cockpit now, sir. What are your orders?"

Marlowe went white and angrily started forward – stopped only by the damning click of a gun being cocked, ready to fire.

With a sickeningly sardonic grin, Shakespeare flicked a switch on the intercom and spoke into it slowly, emphasising every syllable: "Crash it."

As the airship lurched violently, a terrific shudder sending everyone toppling, Marlowe exploded with rage, colour in his face hastening from white to crimson: "Damn you! You said you'd let us live!"

"I lied."

TEN

Chaos erupted as Shakespeare turned on his heel and slipped quickly out of sight. The whole room shuddered with sickening ferocity as above them the massive starboard engine rotor stuttered and died, belching smoke and threatening flame. With the other engine still active and functioning with the power of both engines combined, the room listed precariously. As the big-band and their instruments tumbled sideways, crashing to the floor and sliding towards the walls, the enormous airship curved away from the clear airspace it had been safely occupying and headed slowly in the direction of the City of Oxford. Thick black smoke billowed from the dead motor, giving the impression to those who could see the action from the ground of a bullet rocketing from a gun barrel.

Pinter was quick off the mark. He kissed Lana on the forehead: "Don't go anywhere, I'll be right back."

"Rupert, what the hell are you doing?"

He winked, then crawled out from under the table and

after Shakespeare. He dodged falling cutlery and chairs as they plunged towards him, pushing his way through a maintenance shaft access door – straight into the bowels of the *Carthaginian*. It was a stark contrast to the lushly decorated interiors of the state-rooms and ballrooms, far removed from their imposing hugeness, and instead presenting him with the image he'd had of the floating ship's militaristic nature: corrugated metal, exposed pipes and thin, dank, claustrophobic corridors.

Pinter undid his bow tie and unbuttoned the top two buttons of his dress shirt, cursing his luck that he'd left his Webley at home and his blindness to the obviously dubious nature of the safety of the party.

Damn it all to hell, he thought. *Why does this keep happening to me?*

Up ahead he spotted Shakespeare, jogging towards a ladder leading up into the heart of the balloon. He seemed to be having a leisurely time of this all, not particularly bothered about making a swift escape. Pinter guessed that he had assumed the chaos of a crashing airship would be enough to stop anyone's attempts to pursue him.

He's probably right, but he didn't count on me, he thought to himself. If he pushed himself hard enough he could reach the bugger before Shakespeare got away and hopefully drag him back to Marlowe. Maybe then he'd get some answers. Maybe then he'd find out what on Earth he had gone and got himself wrapped up in.

Pinter almost tripped as a bullet ricocheted off a pipe too close to his head for comfort. Steam hissed from the hole the impact had made and as he spun around he spotted his pursuer, who fired off another poorly aimed shot that struck a pipe with a direct hit and sent searing steam into the tunnel ahead of them, blocking the passageway and cutting him off from Shakespeare completely.

There was no way through.

Fear raced through Pinter's veins. He was at the mercy of the gunman now, and there was nothing he could do.

He murmured to himself: "Oh, shit."

Seeing his prey now cornered and with no way to run, the gunman raised his pistol, walking slowly towards Pinter with a victor's smile plastered all over his face. As his features became clearer with proximity, and the man stepped out of the shadows and into the crimson glow of a red warning light, Pinter realised he'd seen the man before. It was Lawrence, the thug from the mountains, and he seemed to be relishing the moment. Perhaps it was a thing of arrogance, a mark of pride, that he should get the upper-hand on Pinter rather than Roach. Pinter swallowed deeply, raised his arms in defeat and tried the only thing he could: "Can't we talk this through, first?"

Lawrence laughed cruelly and leveled the gun at his head.

"I guess not." Pinter screwed his eyes shut and waited patiently for the end.

Even in the cacophony of noise in the tunnel, against the percussion of hissing pipes and whirring machinery, the low rumble of the engine and of wind rushing past the zeppelin, the hollow click of a Smith and Wesson hitting an empty chamber was deafening.

Without pausing for thought, Pinter charged the man and tackled him. Surprised but stocky, Lawrence held his own and slammed Pinter into the pipes, wrapping his fingers around his neck. Somehow Lawrence found the bow tie and pulled it taut. Gasping for air, Pinter struggled against the raw strength of the man, looking for any point of weakness. Punches to the chest didn't do any good and neither did kicking him in the groin, an area that frankly seemed almost barren. For a second, Rupert was surprised enough to wear a bemused expression before he remembered he was losing air, and fast. It was down to a battle of wills, a combat of strength and strength alone. A fight that Pinter wasn't sure he could win.

The air was burning his lungs trying to escape and Pinter knew he was running out of time. He hadn't had a chance to take a breath before Lawrence had locked his hands around his throat. Realising it was now or never, with Herculean effort he shoved Lawrence backwards, catching him on the wrong foot and swinging the two of them in an arc - directly into the steam rushing through the hole in the pipe beside them.

The shriek was horrific, as Lawrence's skin cooked violently through the thin black shirt he wore. He threw Pinter off him, sending him sprawling to the ground of the previously impassable part of the tunnel.

Clear of the steam.

Lawrence staggered with searing flesh behind the screen of hot air, caught as though he were a marionette puppet of the Hunchback of Notre Dame lit from behind. There was a clatter as he collapsed to the ground, moaning in excruciating pain as his body roasted.

Pinter shrugged off the shock, wiping sweat from his brow and breathing in fresh air deeply. It struck him that the purchase of a new tuxedo for the event was a serious mistake. The sleeves were already stained with oil and the lapels were starting to furrow.

He shook his head clear of vain sartorial thoughts and looked ahead of him. There was only one way to go, and that was onwards and upwards. He stepped up to the ladder and grabbed the first rung.

"Well," he muttered to himself. "Here goes nothing."

**

The reserve pilots had already found their way into the cockpit by the time the zeppelin passed over suburbs of Oxford. Both were experienced mechanics, and it had not taken them long to kick down the door to the cockpit and discover the unconscious bodies of the former pilots slumped in a corner. The wheel rocked helplessly from side to side as the steering fin was battered by up-winds and down-winds produced by the city below. Within moments of taking up the pilot's seat, Seymour had managed to straighten out their course and hold them steady. The starboard engine was still giving them stick and it fell to Benjamin to try and get the rotor up and running. Glancing out of the window, Seymour could see smoke billowing from the disabled rotor-blade and with beads of nervous sweat running down his cheeks he picked up the intercom to contact Marlowe in the state-room above them.

The crackling voice cut through the panicked screams as the room swayed from side to side. Silence descended as Marlowe fought against gravity to answer the call.

"This is Seymour in the pilot's seat, sir. The pilots are alive but out cold. Still having trouble with the starboard engine but we'll keep you posted."

"What's our course as it stands, Mr Seymour?"

There was a long, deathly pause. Then: "If we can't sort out the engine soon...we'll be flying right into Oxford Cathedral."

There was a crash as Reverend Dawkins collapsed in shock. Marlowe felt his blood run cold. "Do your best, gentlemen. Do your very best."

ELEVEN

As soon as he pulled himself clear of the hatch that opened into the main chamber of the super-structure, Pinter felt the pressure of air attacking him from all directions. It strained his grip on the thin metal ladder that continued up to the roof of the balloon and forced him to steel himself against the onslaught. Some way above him, in the middle of the balloon, the ladder reached a platform that stretched across the length of the balloon interior and through the ring-doughnut shaped gas-bags; massive internal balloons filled with helium.

It was a very long, very thin, very dangerous platform.

Oh, great. Just what I need, Pinter thought. He swallowed heavily and gripped the rungs of the ladder tighter. Carefully, he forced himself slowly higher, hand over hand over hand, all too aware that every step up meant a considerably more dangerous fall. For a moment he thought he'd lost his grip, and he clutched the rungs with all his might, his knuckles going white from strain and his heart beating firmly against his teeth.

Don't look down, Rupert, he willed himself. *Just don't look down.*

Above him, Shakespeare seemed to have noticed he was being followed. With a distant but evident grin he waved happily at his pursuer, holding on with one hand as strong winds battered him from side to side and whipped his oiled hair into a frenzy.

Pinter watched in disbelief. The man was impossible.

Shaking his head, he forced himself to press on. He was gaining now, catching up more quickly than he'd assumed he would, as Shakespeare was taking his time and gently hauling himself up onto the platform.

Pinter's arms burned as though they were on fire and more than anything he wanted just to lie down for a moment and catch his breath.

No such luck.

By the time Shakespeare could be bothered to climb to a stand on the platform Pinter was within reaching distance. Imagining his prey was as tired as he was, Pinter figured that hurrying and grabbing him while he rested was the best option. He pulled himself over the ledge and looked up into the cheerful face before him.

"Hello!" The words were said without a hint of malice and for a moment Pinter considered that he'd gotten Shakespeare all wrong.

What shattered the illusion was the boot colliding brutally with his jaw and sending him tumbling backwards, back over the edge and into oblivion.

Scrambling for a handhold, Pinter found a horrible moment where he hung practically upside down, looking below him at a severe drop. His bow tie, already loose from the fight with Lawrence, slipped off and whipped downwards into the nether, twirling in the wind. He shouted in pain as his arm bore the full force of his body weight falling and for a chilling moment he thought he'd broken the bone.

Don't be a fool, he told himself. *If it was broken, you'd be heading for the bottom of the balloon by now.*

He dragged himself back onto the ladder proper, climbing back to the platform and peering over first to check if Shakespeare was lying in wait to deliver another, this time more decisive, kick to the face. Certain that he could reach safety without hindrance this time, Pinter climbed over and onto the platform.

Steadying himself, he wiped blood from his mouth and stood upright, swaying slightly in the breeze that swept through the colossal belly of the airship. The platform was broad enough for the width of a man and a half to stand comfortably, but the perilous drop either side was prevented only by a thin strip of metal that acted as a railing.

Nice and safe, he thought. *And plenty of room, too.*

At intervals along the length of the platform, positioned just before it passed through the circular space at the centre of each of the six gas-bags, were upright ladders on a locked swing. He imagined that it was to allow the ladders to interchange between vertical and horizontal positions for maintenance on the balloon. At the far end of the platform was an access door to the exterior of the aircraft's tail, and it was towards this that Shakespeare now jogged as fast as he could, checking over his shoulder periodically to calculate the distance between them. He was barely half way to his escape route.

Pinter took off, sprinting behind him and aiming to grab Shakespeare before he could get away. He was close now, and all it would take was a carefully positioned rugby tackle. As long as they didn't pitch sideways and tumble off the platform, of course.

Shakespeare however, having seen Pinter get to his feet and take off after him, pre-empted the attack. As Rupert reached him he planted his heel firmly to the floor and spun 180 degrees, facing Pinter head on and delivering a tremendous punch to the gut that the younger man couldn't evade. The impact of the ensuing collision sent the two crashing heavily into the railing. They watched as the Luger in Shakespeare's holster tumbled into the abyss below. As Pinter fought for breath in his winded lungs, Shakespeare tried to pull himself out of the grapple verbally: "You seem to have a habit of showing up at inappropriate times. Who are you? I've forgotten your name."

"Rupert Pinter." The reply was barely a rasp as he fought for his breath.

"Pinter? How quaint. You're sticking your nose in where it doesn't belong."

"I'm good at that."

Catching him off guard, Pinter struck a clean blow to Shakespeare's jaw, sending him back the way they'd come. With his escape compromised, Shakespeare now attacked with ferocity, but gradually and through sheer determination Pinter forced him back towards the ladder they'd climbed as they traded blows. Pinter seemed to have the greater level of conviction as he drove Shakespeare back, not giving the man any ground as they stumbled closer and closer. They were within spitting distance of death when Shakespeare finally turned the tables, forcing Pinter around so that his back faced their ascension ladder, no more than a footstep away from the precipice. Lining up a punch, Shakespeare threw his fist at Pinter's head, who, in ducking the blow, revealed an exhausted and badly burnt Lawrence. The man had dragged himself painfully up in the time the two men had been fighting, and was immediately knocked backwards by Shakespeare's blow – screaming as he plummeted to his eventual, if prolonged, death.

For a moment Shakespeare and Pinter shared a surprised and morbidly amused look as he fell, before Shakespeare broke the mood with another heavy punch to the jaw that sent Pinter spinning into the railing, bringing his arms up in a boxers pose to block the next blow.

**

Far below, in the cockpit, Benjamin struggled with the electrics, blanketed in a cloud smoke and the popping of sparks. From the shroud around him, he could hear Seymour yelling: "Ben, you should look at this!"

The panic is his voice was unmistakable, and as Benjamin glanced over, a terrifying sight loomed ahead. They were on a direct course with the steeple of Oxford Cathedral.

"Oh, Christ!" Benjamin leapt over to the engine control and fought frantically with the wires. Sweat dropped in bucket-loads from his forehead as the steeple drew closer and closer.

"We're running out of air..." Seymour had fixed his eyes forward. His pupils were like needle-points and he gritted his teeth, anticipating the end.

With a massive spark that launched Seymour to the other side of the cockpit and a rumble that caused the entire airship to shudder, the starboard engine kicked in. As the pressure on the throttle released the zeppelin pitched suddenly upwards, catching the underside on the tip of the steeple and sending a shockwave rippling through the airship. It caused no immediate damage, but the congregation in the ballroom tumbled all over the place as the floor became almost vertical.

Above them, the shockwave rushed through the stomach of the aircraft, knocking a grappling Pinter and Shakespeare onto a maintenance ladder, which in turn, with a sickening creak as the sturdy metal bent under the sudden pressure, plummeted downwards, taking the two men with it.

TWELVE

When Pinter opened his eyes he found himself suspended above the sharp drop by his fingertips, hanging onto the now horizontal ladder. Opposite was Shakespeare, who winked at him before motioning comically below and rolling his eyes theatrically.

The breeze whipped between his knees, causing him to sway gently from side to side. Whatever had just happened, it couldn't have been good...but they were still alive, so he assumed that it could have been infinitely worse. He dared not look down, but when his curiosity got the better of him his heart leapt into his mouth and he found himself releasing a guttural mutter: "Well...that's not good. That isn't good at all."

"Quite the position we're in, eh?" Shakespeare's tone still held the constant joviality it had before and Pinter considered that maybe the man was completely and utterly mad.

"What do you want?"

"I'm a businessman. This is my business."

"It's a dangerous business!"

Shakespeare feigned a shrug, despite their position: "It pays well." He pulled himself up slowly onto the ladder and found his footing on the rungs, then scrambled back across and onto the platform. As he lifted himself to his feet, he brushed himself off, looking down almost pityingly at Pinter: "I'd offer you a hand up, but I'd be worried you'd do something foolish. Trying to hinder me and my purposes further, for example. As such, while it pains me to have to do it, old chap..." he kicked the bolted clamp at the end of the ladder, loosening it further: "...I'm going to have to leave you hanging around for a bit. Hope you don't mind!"

The ladder lurched perilously downwards, metal creaking under the strain of Pinter's weight. He held his tongue as Shakespeare laughed viciously before slowly sauntering along the platform to the hatch at the end of the airship. He still had quite a way to go, but was content in the knowledge that his final action had secured him plenty of time to get away.

Pinter took a deep breath. His fingers, which shook with fright, were slipping from the ladder and the dull groan of dying metal deafened him. His heart raced.

It was a hell of a drop.

Don't look down, he told himself. He hated heights at the best of times, but this was really taking the biscuit. It struck him that maybe this wasn't the greatest idea he'd ever had. *Next time, I'm keeping my feet firmly on the ground.*

He shuddered.

If there is a next time.

As steadily as he could, Pinter shifted his weight sideways so that he could hang from the end of the ladder. Grasping the rung tightly, he braced himself as the ladder bent further, taking him to a completely vertical hang.

Now it was just a case of climbing to safety. It all seemed simple enough.

The easy part.

Pinter allowed himself a grin, which was instantly wiped from his face as the ladder shuddered violently and a bolt dropped past his head, spinning endlessly towards the bottom of the balloon. It fell for a long time, longer than Pinter cared to watch it for. He went white and suddenly all thoughts of caution disappeared. There was nothing for it – he had to hurry now. If he didn't, he could end up going the same way. He used all his effort to scramble up the ladder.

As his hand grasped the edge of the platform, gripping it tightly, he felt the ladder fall away beneath him. His heart skipped a beat as he realised that his tuxedo jacket was tangled in one of the rungs. Holding on for dear life, he felt the weight of the ladder try to drag him down as fabric tore with a sickening rip. The ladder disappeared below, clutching a section of his new tuxedo in its metal jaws as it fell.

Pinter gave himself a moment to catch his breath on the relative safety of the platform, lying on his chest and watching the ladder fall. It struck the bottom of the balloon and bounced before it clattered. Marlowe had been right after all – British engineered zeppelins were sturdy indeed. He'd half expected the ladder to pass straight through the balloon...which would have made matters even worse. He sighed in relief before pushing himself to his feet.

His body ached all over, bruised nastily already from the barrage of punches Shakespeare had delivered.

The fellow has a decent right hook, Pinter considered as he rubbed his chin, feeling blood dripping from a graze beneath his bottom lip. He felt the tooth he'd almost lost in the mountains hanging loose again, but it was nothing a decent dentist couldn't handle. It would simply mean another reprimand from Mr Dalton about the necessity of oral care.

Ahead of him he spotted Shakespeare, who was now crawling through the access hatch, heading out onto the tail of the aircraft. With adrenaline pumping through his veins Pinter sprinted after him, ignoring the soreness of his joints and focusing on getting back on the mercenary's tail. He reached the access panel a few moments after Shakespeare had gone through, and dropped to his knees to follow him outside.

He couldn't help but gasp as he emerged on the other side. He stood now on the rear fin of the airship, the Oxford skyline disappearing into the distance. It was obvious that they'd gotten clear of the city by now. Even from this distance he was able to make out the damage to the steeple of the Cathedral, which bent limply in the lights of the city, bowing in shame. A trail of smoke hung in the air, shrouding the Cathedral and displaying all too clearly the course they'd taken. He shook his head in wonder. How close they'd come.

Sheltered by the bulk of the *Carthaginian*, the wind wasn't too bad, but even still Pinter held onto the safety rung of the hatch. He could only watch as Shakespeare nodded in appreciation of the effort, saluted quickly, gave him a wink, then leapt from the aircraft, his parachute joining those of his comrades a few short moments later.

Rupert Pinter gritted his teeth. He had a bad feeling about Bill Shakespeare and with both the Dagda Cauldron and Sword of Nuada in his grasp there remained only two of the four mythical treasures. If, indeed, they were more than just a myth.

"I'd better get to the library!" He shouted after

Shakespeare. "And find out what exactly you're up to!"

He collected his thoughts and ducked back inside the airship. Now that the flow of adrenaline had stopped, he felt the pain all at once. He set his sights ahead, and limped back to the ballroom - and hopefully to safety - as the floodlights of the zeppelin mooring site glared ahead of them.

**

Lana was the first to spot a badly bruised Pinter emerging from the maintenance door and when she did she threw herself at him, wrapping her arms around him tightly and burying her head in his shoulder. Though the affection was reassuring and he returned it without hesitation, Pinter winced in pain as she crushed his already injured body with more ferocity. She let him go as he let out a pained cough.

"Where the hell did you go? I was worried sick!"

"Upstairs." He slumped into a vacant chair as the airship began its descent.

She knelt beside him, placing her hand in his and squeezing it tight. "Who was he?"

"I don't know," Pinter muttered. "But I'm starting to dislike him."

"What happened?"

"Not a lot. All in good sport, as far as he's concerned, I'm sure."

"You look terrible, Rupert. Look at you...your clothes are ruined and you're covered in blood. What did I tell you about being more careful?"

"You should see the other guy." He grinned and despite the alarm still clear in her sparkling grey eyes, Lana managed to return the smile and rested her head on his shoulder. He tenderly kissed her forehead: "Don't worry about me. I'm fine. Just a bit shaken up. I hate heights."

The airship rumbled as the mooring cables pulled taut and Pinter got painfully to his feet. With a great deal of care, he slipped the remains of his tuxedo jacket from his arms and draped it over Lana's shoulders as the collected mass made their way to the disembarkation ramp. He rolled his sleeves up and swung his braces off. He didn't give a damn now if it wasn't the right thing for the company they were in. His trousers weren't going to fall down, the extra belt he always wore made sure of that. He just wanted to be comfortable for a moment.

Marlowe, naturally, was furious. While Pinter lit Lana's cigarette as they evacuated the airship and stood on the grass beneath the *Carthaginian Storm*, her father's cheeks fluctuated between a dark crimson and light purple. He chewed the end of a cigar ferociously and spat out his words: "This is an outrage! Who the hell was that fellow?"

"He said his name was Shakespeare."

"I heard his bloody name!" Marlowe tore into the unfortunate lackey who'd managed to innocently patronise him and now cowered in fear before a smoking volcano: "I want answers! I want to know who he was and what the hell he wants with the artifact! We've risked too much to lose it. It thought we stepped up security after what happened in Istanbul?"

"Steps were taken, sir." The man's voice shook. Pinter tried to hide back a smile when he realised that the man was nothing more than a personal assistant, who had nothing to do with security or protocol, and whose sole purpose in Marlowe's entourage was to take notes and file memos.

"Obviously not nearly enough of them! And Mr Pinter...!"

Rupert froze, his ears burning as though a hot poker had

been placed upon them. As if this evening wasn't bad enough already. "Yes, sir?"

"Well done for giving chase. You're a good chap, Rupert. Your father would have been quite proud."

"Thank you, sir." The relief flowed through him.

Marlowe stepped over to them, shooing away his assistant and looking Pinter up and down. "You do look terrible, though, I must say. Must've been quite a scrap with that Shakespeare fellow. In the rafters of the bloody place as well, I understand. Dangerous business. Any other father would assume you have a death wish and wouldn't want you anywhere near his daughter." He smiled broadly as Pinter's arm dropped away from Lana and he took a step back. "Of course, I'm not any other father. Will you join me for that drink, now?"

"It'd be an honour, sir."

Lana gave Pinter a knowing wink. "See. I told you he likes you."

THIRTEEN

Though his head swam with blurred memories of too much whiskey, lavish estate rooms and what he hoped was paternal acceptance, Pinter traversed the marble stairs of the Oxford University History Library with speed and ease, pausing only at the top to gaze down at the foyer. It was adorned with tastefully placed statues, no doubt imported from the luxurious collections of the British Museum, and gave the building a grandeur that left him feeling proud, if anything, to be a member of the University.

It was still early in the morning so the halls were vacant, except for the receptionist, who sat with her head buried in a ledger and had barely glanced up as Pinter strode through the doors. This was the way he preferred it. The library gave him the sense of solitude he needed to think clearly, and he'd found the best way to vent his frustration was not over a gin and tonic and rant at the Daggers Club but rather by burying his nose in a book - a trait he'd learnt only too well from his father. As such, the library seemed like a second home.

He gradually made his way through art encrusted corridors to the Celtic History and Archaeology section, a dark and quiet area of the library that was almost permanently devoid of life. Though Randle and Tirey had both managed to stimulate a good deal more interest in the subject than the University was used to, it was one of the criteria of studies that students tended to avoid unless they had a vested interest in the topic. Even Pinter often found the subject tiresome, even though his exposure was limited to the study of Celtic languages in his linguistics classes.

Today, however, a single lamp gave the chamber a strange orange glow and the shadow of Geoffrey Randle cast a haggard silhouette on the wall. His normally trimmed beard was unkempt and his eyes appeared almost hollow, the harsh light accentuating his sunken features. He sat hunched over a thick, dusty tome, his free hand running through thicker, dustier hair – greyer too than Pinter recalled. It had obviously been a tough few weeks for the old man. *Not surprising really, given the circumstances*, Pinter told himself.

"I thought I'd find you here."

The professor's head snapped to attention, caught off guard for a moment. He relaxed when he saw Pinter, and managed a pained but defeated smile: "I saw the papers this morning. I imagine you had an eventful evening with the Marlowe family?"

"That's one word for it."

Randle sighed: "Shakespeare?"

"That's another word. Who else would it have been?"

Randle nodded slowly. "I see. I've been doing some research on the fellow. Do you have any idea who he is?"

"Enlighten me," Pinter said, slipping off his hat and leaning against one of the towering bookshelves: "No-one else seems to be able to."

"He was one of Tirey's students...once upon a time. He was expelled from the University a few years ago for cheating on a test."

"Expelled for cheating? That's something of an overreaction, don't you think?"

"On the contrary, he tried to blackmail an examiner, and when the poor chap refused, threatened him with a Luger instead."

Pinter snorted: "Well, if you're going to cheat..."

"...might as well do it in style?" Randle finished with a morbid grin. "Quite. This explains his interest in the Dagda Cauldron. Tirey obviously didn't trust him, so he had the old man bumped off."

"It seems so. Anything else on him?"

"Some strange affiliations. The Conservative Party, the Rotary Club. He comes from money, that much is evident. But I can't find out anything else. It's almost as though he one day just came into being. The University has tried to deny that the whole affair ever happened. Which leaves us in a tough spot." His head fell into his hands: "If only Tirey had told me about the bugger we could have been more careful. I must've missed him by a matter of weeks."

"How do you mean?"

"I was still looking for your father in China. I must've returned to the University after my sabbatical just after they expelled Shakespeare. Tirey obviously never talked about the whole business because he was too ashamed of it."

"What about these 'Four Treasures' he stole?" Pinter took the initiative to steer the conversation away from past scars. The dead were dead, and he didn't like to dwell on them – for both of their sakes.

"Three of four, so far."

"Three? I thought it was only two? The Sword of

Nuada and the Dagda Cauldron? What happened to the third?"

"They got the Stone of Fal a year ago."

"That's in broad daylight!"

"Was in broad daylight," Randle sighed. "It disappeared last year. People assumed it was a prank, but it never came back. This makes sense, though."

"How does it make sense? How can it possibly make sense?" Pinter's eyes were wide now, his voice rising. From somewhere down the hall, somebody hissed for him to be quiet.

"By the line that connects the points, my boy."

"Which would be?" Randle closed the tome and showed Pinter the cover in its moth-bitten entirety. He shrugged: "Druids?"

"Not the bog-standard pagans-in-a-park druids, Rupert. Dark magic, occult obsessed, would-be sorcerers. The real wizards-of-old."

"That's crazy." Pinter took a seat across from his mentor and took the book, looking it over. "You're seriously telling me that our man Bill is working for a cult?"

"That would be my summary, yes."

Pinter sat back in his chair for a moment. Littering the desk were newspaper cuttings, among them the article about the stolen Stone of Fal. One cutting in particular caught his eye: "'Strange Happenings in Stonehenge'? You *are* being serious..." he said, limply.

"Of course. And that's not the scary thing."

"What is?"

Randle's voice dropped low and took on a whisper: "How much do you know about the Tuatha De Danann?"

Pinter drew his seat in closer "Just what you told me in Wales. They were a cult that settled in Ireland. The very core of the Four Treasures myth."

Randle nodded: "As I told you before, most scholars believe that the Tuatha De Danann has about as much resonance as a creation myth. The primary source-work is poetry, which makes it about as likely as Odysseus and the Cyclops. But as you've seen, there may be more fact to the fiction here. The Tuatha De were perhaps a collection of early Druids, learned in the dark arts and in magic. They collected together in Ireland having experienced and exodus from four islands, 'four corners of the Earth'. The people who came from the island of Murias brought forth the Dagda Cauldron. The people of Findas brought the Sword of Nuada. Those of Falias brought the Stone of Fal, and there was one more."

"The Spear of Lug?" Pinter asked, positive of the answer this time. He'd done his homework.

"Well remembered. The Spear of Lug, often mistaken for the Spear of Destiny. Two very similar spears, two very different stories."

"So what if Shakespeare has all these treasures? What's the best he can do? Sell them? Fill a Druid-fancier's collection with ancient relics of mythological power? It's nonsense."

"If all these items were brought together, I suppose one could surmise the resurrection of the Tuatha De Danann."

"So there'll be even *more* druids?"

"More than just druids. Twisted by their own dark magic, they destroyed themselves. Those three Druid priests I told you about, who fled to the British Isles, were trying to protect their people from themselves. If they are resurrected..." Randle trailed off, forlorn. "Well, it wouldn't be good, I can tell you that much."

You've got to be joking, Pinter thought. "This is all nonsense, Dr Randle-"

"Geoffrey. You've known me long enough, and I'm not

a tenured professor anymore."

"-Geoffrey. Utter nonsense. These stories are just that – stories. The 'magic powers' are hocus pocus."

"Do you remember what I told you back in the Passage of the Dancers, Rupert?"

"You told me that it was all a question of whether you feel the need to believe in something."

Randle smiled: "And I'm as skeptical as you, believe me. But this fellow Shakespeare seems determined enough to risk life and limb for a 'mere' myth. Surely even as a skeptic this is enough to give you the drive to find out what this really means? What these treasures really stand for? We could unlock a mystery of the past, see for ourselves the divine without having to question it."

There was a long moment as Pinter ran this through his mind. Randle was right – there was something strange about the Cauldron when he'd touched it. Something unworldly. Something that made him want to know more.

This was an opportunity too good to miss, one he'd been waiting long enough for. The chance for some answers. He smiled: "So what do we do?"

"I imagine they'll be after the instrument of the people of Gorias, for starters. The Spear of Lug, lost for centuries."

"Then a better question is where do we start? This Spear could be anywhere."

Randle could only smile at Pinter's excitement. "I know a man in Monte Carlo. A man named Christoph Chaucer."

"Will he help us?"

"We can only hope. If anyone can help us get the spear before Shakespeare and the druids then its Christoph. We haven't spoken in almost ten years...not since he was blacklisted for these outrageous claims...but I'm sure he'll be more than happy to help as soon as he finds out about what's been going on while he's been cooped up in the Riviera."

Pinter jumped to his feet. "I'll pack my bag. We can get a train to Dover, and then on to LeHavre by boat. It'll take us a day or two to get there overland by train but if we set off tonight we should have a decent head-start."

"I'll meet you at the station."

Pinter nodded, collected his things and left. Randle sat for a moment in the near dark, fingering a musty page between his index finger and thumb and listening to the distant tolling of the Cathedral bells calling the Sunday parishioners to prayer. He yawned, suddenly aware of the time. He'd been tirelessly scanning books all night, and the fatigue was gaining on him fast. His leg was starting to hurt as well, a by-product of not resting it.

It was odd that the ache had come at now of all times, almost as though Rupert acted as a severe reminder of his father. He was the spitting image of the young Alexander Pinter, filled with the child-like excitement of an adolescent but with the sensibility and eyes of someone much older.

He cast his mind to the trenches of Hell, the horrible day when he'd first met Alexander Pinter properly as he tended to his wounded leg. They knew each other from the Daggers Club, all that time ago. Forgotten faces lost in a world of despair, but yet giving such comfort at the end of the world. They became best friends from the moment they'd started chatting, despite never really having much to do with each other in their days at Oxford. Fate does strange things, but throwing Randle, Pinter and Tirey back together was one of the better destinies.

What a day that had been. Randle had thought he'd bought it. A lot of men had at the Somme.

Look at me now, Alexander, he thought morbidly. *So much for looking after the boy. I'm putting him in even more danger.*

His mind returned to the present then, to the danger that lay ahead. There was something about this that scared him and he couldn't quite put his finger on it.

FOURTEEN

Fresh sea air acted as a remedy for the dregs of the hangover. With a cup of milky tea in his hand, Pinter leant on the railing of the clipper, watching Dover Harbour vanish in the wash of the boat as it raced towards the French Riviera, the white cliffs glowing radiantly in the corner of his eye. The journey ahead was to be a dull one, he imagined. Being cooped up first in a boat and then on a train for hours on end was hardly his idea of fun, but it would simply have to be a case of waiting it out. They would play cards and watch the waves break behind the small boat. Then they would watch the world rushing by in a cloak of steam as they raced southwards.

Randle stepped up beside him wordlessly, removing his trilby – an uncomfortable replacement for his lost Australian hunting hat – and placing his hand on his shoulder. He smiled at first with paternal pride, but it wasn't long before his brow creased and his expression became pained: "I have a bad feeling about this, Rupert."

"Join the club," Pinter murmured. He turned to face the old man: "What's the plan for when we get to Monte Carlo?"

Randle shrugged: "There are a few haunts that Chaucer frequents. I suppose we ought to try those first."

"He's a man of habit then?"

"Unfortunately, yes."

"Drink?"

"And gambling. Quite a great deal of both, in fact."

Pinter couldn't help but roll his eyes: "Wonderful. So we're dealing with a drunk who was laughed out of academic society because of his outlandish insistence that this myth was real. I'm waiting for you to tell me that Atlantis is involved in all of this..."

"...well..." Randle winked, breaking Pinter's sarcastic mood. The younger man couldn't help but smile, and shook his head:

"Will he actually be lucid enough to help us?"

"We can only hope. He only really descended into drink and high stakes poker when his expedition to search for the Spear of Lug fell through. He asked for ridiculous volumes of money and brought no proof...or even suitable evidence, in fact...to the table. He became something of a running joke between academics. If someone misunderstood a reference or a quote, they'd 'pulled a Chaucer.' Historians can be crueler than children sometimes. The lack of funding and suggestion of his mental state being in deterioration ruined him." Randle sighed, as if anticipating his own destiny: "He was a brilliant man, destroyed by economics."

"Aren't they all?"

The old man laughed distantly. "I suppose so. And for the record, Rupert, when we travel back we're going by plane. I should have enough funds to buy us a flight on a tri-motor out of Monaco. I hate boats. Absolutely hate them. Is that clear?"

Pinter smiled and nodded: "Crystal clear."

The sun had started to sink by the time the English Coast had disappeared from sight, painting the sky a pastel orange. Grey clouds permeated the otherwise flawless strokes of colour across the canvas of the horizon. Randle said his farewells and disappeared inside the boat, but Pinter remained on deck until the sun set completely, his brown flat cap mashed tightly onto his skull to prevent it from whipping off his head and plunging into the froth below.

He stared out to sea, watching as the stars began to blink to life and the orange sky faded to dark purple. Part of him wished he'd never signed up to the Dagda Expedition. It would have prevented a great deal of heartache, with essays due in a matter of weeks, none of which he'd started – and here he was on a boat bound for the south of France instead of attending lectures.

Perhaps it was that that thrilled him, because deep down he knew he was having the time of his life. Pinter grinned to himself. Night was closing in as he opened the door to the cabins, taking one last, long draw of sea air into his lungs before ducking inside.

Don't be so hasty to write this all off, he told himself as the first stars appeared. *It's barely even begun.*

Roach Lestate was rather pleased with the blindness of the old man and the boy. Even though he appeared quite different in a grey pin-stripe suit, with a hat pulled down low over his eyes, he had one of those unmistakably weathered faces that stood out in a crowd. His skin had the appearance of an old map, torn and creased and pock-marked, lined by the scars that covered his face from a thousand fights. Once Pinter had ducked back inside, he lowered his newspaper and rose from the bench that he had occupied for long enough to kill all feeling in his legs. It was lucky that he was relatively simple-minded, otherwise the hours sat reading the same article in an old newspaper would have been a seemingly endless hell. The benefit, he told himself, was that he now knew in detail all the most recent news stories. He'd be great at a pub quiz.

He proceeded directly to the telegram office, taking a seat and dropping a bundle of carefully wrapped ten pound notes on the cashier's lap before beginning his message to his employer:

TRAIL WARM STOP WILL CONTINUE STOP CHRISTOPH CHAUCER STOP TRAIN ARRIVES MONTE CARLO MORNING STOP ROACH FULL STOP

It would only be a matter of time before Shakespeare collected the telegram, and even less time before the chartered bi-plane would be prepared to leave. The speed of the plane would mean that Shakespeare would most likely arrive in Monte Carlo shortly after they did.

Roach chuckled to himself. Shakespeare was right. This was too easy.

Far too easy.

FIFTEEN

The estate of Christoph Chaucer was extravagant. The modest farm house was surrounded by acres of land, wild Riviera countryside tamed into ordered and beautiful gardens that stretched out of sight towards the coast. For a man in a bad financial position, it seemed that Chaucer was all too aware of the equity in his house to give it up. Pinter wasn't surprised – it was an enviable property.

The small car Randle had collected at the station, an aging, red Citroen Type A that rattled and spluttered as it trundled through the country lanes, drew to a halt at the end of the long driveway with a rumble, stirring Pinter from an uncomfortable nap. He lifted his flat cap from over his eyes and yawned heavily before following Randle and climbing out into the gorgeous sunshine. He whistled as he took the view in. The cottage had a magnificent view of the gardens as they rolled towards the dramatic cliffs.

"Quite a house."

Randle nodded: "Christoph has always had a taste for

the exquisite, and has been an excellent horticulturalist since I've known him. You probably wouldn't be surprised that he kept bees for a time."

"For a time?"

"He realised only once he'd invested in the equipment that he didn't actually like honey in the slightest."

Pinter laughed. "A neurotic historian. Who would have thought?"

Randle could only shrug in amused defeat before leading the way down a small pathway to the front door of the cottage. As he raised his fist to knock, the door creaked gently open before him.

"That's odd." He turned to Pinter, his concern evident.

Pinter's hand went immediately to his holster, and he quietly drew and cocked his Webley as Randle slowly pushed the door open fully.

The house was silent, deathly so. Occasionally the chirping of a bird cut through the air, or the light wind hissed and whistled through the windows, but the world seemed to have come to a complete standstill. Even the roaring current of the distant ocean was lost in the emptiness. Pinter moved slowly from room to room, noticing one consistent thing – the place was chaos. Tables had been overturned, drawers emptied and folders scattered. The house had been completely ransacked, and Chaucer was nowhere to be found.

Certain the house was empty, Pinter holstered his revolver and yelled to Randle: "No sign of him anywhere. Where on earth do you think he is?"

"I've no idea, but I'll admit that I'm starting to become worried."

Pinter's skin crawled. What if they were too late? What if Shakespeare and his men had pre-empted them and already snatched Chaucer from their grasp?

He stepped through the doorway and into Chaucer's room and almost immediately flushed with relief: "I think I've found him."

Randle stumbled in: "Where?"

Motioning to the open wardrobe, he spoke through air thick with the scent of cheap French cologne: "He's at a Casino. And if I'm right..." he held up a membership card, bent out of shape and scruffy from what could only be assumed was too much time spent discarded in a jacket pocket: "The Casino Paradise Lost. Appropriate enough. This looks like a membership card."

"Good boy!"

"Come on. Let's get down there before it gets dark. With any luck we can stop him before he loses too much money."

Roach met Shakespeare at the train station, nervously and unsuccessfully trying to blend into the throng of people in the crowded ticket office until he was satisfied that the correct locomotive was disembarking. His employer had no such pedantic qualms, stepping off the first class carriage of *Le Train Bleu* with an unmistakable air of authority about him. He was well rested and had travelled in the utmost style, as was the way with the luxury locomotive. He was secretly a touch disappointed that his company hadn't included royalty on the journey from Paris to Monaco. That would have given his list of clientele a wonderful boost.

Roach took his suitcase and shook his hand as they met: "Good man, Roach. Sorry about the delay. I had a meeting in Paris that acquired my attention."

"Sir?"

"Dinner with a rather lovely girl, who had a rather lovely business opportunity for us. But all in good time. Do you have any idea where Christoph Chaucer is?"

"None as yet, but I'm sure Pinter and Randle will lead us to him."

Shakespeare nodded, and led their way off the platform and into the station. "Very good. I've no doubt that that loon will be thrilled to see us. The old man and a boy haven't been a problem, have they?"

"No, sir. I'd imagine they suspect we're close behind, but they have no idea I was following them the entire way. I even sat at the table next to them at breakfast and they didn't recognise me. Spent far too much time reading academic journals and talking shop. It was deathly dull."

"Develop some form of cultural awareness, please, old man. That is rather odd, though. You have one of those faces, Roach. No offense."

"None taken, sir. Perhaps they simply weren't looking for me?"

"That old fool Randle ought to have kept his wits about him. Was he carrying his cane?"

"He uses a cane?" Roach's face twisted with confusion.

Shakespeare rubbed his chin. "Interesting. Very interesting indeed. This could be more difficult that we've given it credit. Perhaps we've found adversaries worth the time it'll take to get rid of them." He glanced at the station clock as they passed below it, entranced for a moment by its delicate gold patterns. "It's getting rather more late than I thought. I think we ought to find a cafe and collect our thoughts. Nobody does coffee like the French. Even the Italians don't come close."

Roach nodded: "Of course. The car is waiting outside, sir."

"Well done, Mr Lestate. You're proving your worthiness to be quite considerable."

They strolled steadily through the terminal to the car

Shakespeare had pulled quite a few strings to acquire – a brand new Talbot 105 in black - which sat parked by the main entrance. Roach pitched a dangerous question, but one that had tickled his curiosity since he arrived: "What did they say, Bill? After Oxford?"

"That we've done well, but not done enough. They weren't too happy with the press interest in our little display. Once we have the Spear, I imagine the buggers will relax." Shakespeare's expression was grim: "I just worry that the bargain may change again. We're getting paid well, but not nearly well enough for what they want."

"How do you mean?"

"Never you mind, Roach. It will be dealt with in good time," Shakespeare smiled. "I assure you. Now, I'm starving, and I've heard that the Hotel de Paris has a spectacular menu. Shall we?"

SIXTEEN

The Casino Paradise Lost was, it struck Pinter, a lecherous breeding ground for pious criminals, scum and villainy. He cut through the dense blanket of cigar smoke that hung about the air in endless plumes, resonating from blackjack tables and roulette wheels. In the pit of his belly sat a sense of dread, as though he were prey being stalked in a murky Victorian cobbled alley. He kept his eyes peeled as his body passed through the shroud, other eyes glancing briefly with contempt at him before turning back to their losing hands.

He had no idea what Chaucer looked like, only that Christoph had booked himself into a high-stakes poker game in "The Lucifer Room". That much he'd discovered from a pretty young blonde at the reception, who was suitably impressed with his grasp of the French tongue.

Pinter shrugged off more looks and, coughing on the cigar smoke from a suited baccarat player, sat himself at the bar and ordered a gin and tonic as the house band struck up a jazzy rendition of *Someone to Watch Over Me*. This was destined to be a long evening, and he desperately needed a drink.

As the barman dropped a slice of lime into the tall glass, Pinter addressed him directly: "Seems quite busy in here tonight."

"We are Monte Carlo's premiere casino, sir. We are always busy."

"Heard of a man named Christoph Chaucer? I understand he comes here a lot."

The barman snorted a laugh then placed the glass he was cleaning down and leant casually on the bar: "You are a friend of Mr Chaucer? Or does he owe you money?"

"Perhaps a little of both. I just need a quick talk with him."

"Chaucer is all talk," the man shrugged. "Although by now I would imagine that he can barely talk at all. He had three straight double vodkas before he went in to The Lucifer Room, and with the amount of money he owes the men inside, if he has any teeth left when he returns I will be very surprised indeed."

Great, Pinter thought. *He'll be dead before midnight.* "When will the game end?"

"It will end when it ends."

"Wonderful. I'd better open a tab."

"Your own?"

"Yes." Then he thought for a moment. Smiling at the bartender, he said: "No, scratch that. My drinks are on Mr Chaucer."

"Show card, Mr Cho-sar."

Christoph Chaucer pulled at the collar of his dress shirt and grimaced as the beads of sweat that had accumulated on his thin neck trickled down his spine. The small, angry looking, tuxedoed Chinaman stared with aggressive ferocity: "Today, Mr Cho-sar. I am not a patient man."

"*Mon ami*, there is no need to rush."

"You have-a wasted our time." The Italian voice of Fernando DaCosta, who until now had been sitting quietly in the corner, was filled with venom. DaCosta had made his name selling expensive women to over-paid politicians – an unusual talent for a man who was rumoured to be more interested in members of the same sex for company on cold, dark winter nights. He knew a lot about money, and a lot about losing it and paying heavily for it - evidenced by the long, thin scar that ran from his temple to his chin and that disappeared momentarily behind the eye patch that covered his left eye. He now leant into the single light that illuminated the room and cast their faces into grotesque statues: "Show us-a your cards and give-a me your money."

As the sound of knuckles cracked Chaucer felt the dread fill his body: "Perhaps you would permit me another-"

"Show card!" A high pitched yell in Chinese now. Xiao Huang was accurate in what he'd said – he was not a patient man at the best of times, and in his line of business there was no need to be. That he showed his crooked teeth in the public arena of Monte Carlo had come as something of a surprise to Chaucer. He was notorious in downtrodden circles for defining the art of the Shanghai – he dealt with everything from kidnap to extortion, pedaling opium across the borders into Japan and Russia, and always seemed to be handing out guns to the winning team. When the Bolsheviks had taken Petrograd by storm, it was with a little help behind the scenes from Xiao Huang and his cronies from Peking, who had provided much of the substantial artillery the revolution had used to grasp victory. Not that Huang was a communist himself - he simply defined capitalism in a communist context, and in this instance the revolutionaries had been more generous with their wages.

Chaucer slowly turned his cards over, revealing a pitiful two of hearts and six of clubs. No correlation with other cards. A poorly calculated bluff.

Merde, he thought. *A deadly mistake.*

Crooked teeth shone darkly in the thin light. Xiao Huang had trip aces.

"You pay now."

"*Mon ami...*" he tried to protest. It was no use.

"Now." Leering faces moving in, and fast. Chaucer knew that he was broke and dead drunk. A skirmish would be a short one and knowing his luck, he'd simply end up completely dead.

"Gentlemen," he slurred, "you will understand that I do not bring my money to town. Allow me to write you a –"

"-check? I think-a not."

"You pay. Now."

"*Mon dieu, mes amis!*"

"You are no friend," came a thick, brutish German voice from the opposite end of the table. "You are a liar, a cheat and a bastard." The poker chips took flight as the table toppled over. The hulking Deutsch machine stepped closer. "You will pay us what you owe us. In full."

There was a crack as his knuckles formed a menacing fist and Chaucer pushed himself back in his seat. The German pulled his arm back, preparing to deliver a damning blow to the Frenchman's skull, wrapping fat fingers around his collar to hold him in place. Chaucer closed his eyes.

The revolver sat on his shoulder clicked as the hammer was cocked.

"Take a step back, Hans. You're getting terribly close."

The German paused for a moment, a bemused look painted around a thick moustache.

Chaucer went white as Pinter, hidden in the darkness, continued: "We're all going to be very adult about this, now. Everyone against the back wall or I'll blow Jerry's brains out of the back of his skull."

Slowly the gamblers complied, moving to the back wall with their arms raised. Pinter pulled Chaucer out of his chair quickly and pushed him to the door before focusing his attention on the collection of rogues who stood in the shadows: "Most kind, gentlemen. Most kind."

At that, he high-tailed it, slamming the door behind it and jamming the handle shut with a chair that lay nearby. Chaucer stumbled all over the place, and with a firm grip Pinter swung him up onto his back. The professor was thin and gangly and even as dead-weight was light enough for Pinter to carry him easily.

Within moments they were at the door, strange looks meeting them all the way. The image of a young man carrying an old drunk one was amusing, but after a few drinks and a few losing hands it seemed to some to suggest an omen of sorts. Pinter simply smiled at a concerned bouncer as he passed: "Too much to drink."

A typically French uninterested shrug saw him through the glass double doors and outside to the half moon driveway populated by expensive cars and rich patrons of the Paradise Lost Casino. With an embarrassing rattle, the Citroen bounded into view, and Randle pushed open the door as he rolled past. Pinter took a step, throwing Chaucer into the back, where he curled up in a ball and fell asleep, before he climbed into the passenger seat.

"Trouble?" Randle asked, seeming to be unsure whether to laugh or be concerned.

"He's blind drunk and in serious debt. And could have gotten me killed in there. The company he keeps is far from friendly."

"Wonderful." Randle grimaced and floored it, taking off into the night.

In the passenger seat of the Talbot, which was parked inconspicuously across the road, Roach smiled to himself. He took a sip of malt whiskey from his hip flask and nodded to his driver, who slowly pulled away from the kerb and followed Randle's car at a safe distance, as they wound along the twisty cliff-edge road, out of town and away from the twinkling lights of Monte Carlo.

SEVENTEEN

The morning brought clear blue skies and sun that streamed in through lace curtains. Pinter stirred from his restless slumber slowly. His neck was in agony from a night on the uncomfortable, gaudy velvet chez-lounge that sat at the centre of Chaucer's sitting room. The birdsong of the countryside filled his ears. Gently, he lifted himself from the makeshift bed, buttoning his shirt and pulling his braces over his shoulders before stretching his arms out to their full span. The grandfather clock in the corner of the room told him two things – firstly that it was just past 8 in the morning, and secondly that he'd had about four hours sleep. Getting Chaucer home had taken considerably longer than they'd thought.

He slipped on his shoes and wandered out of the lounge into the kitchen, where he groggily splashed some icy water on his face from the faucet, deciding that it was the closest he'd get to some form of normality. He noticed voices drifting in through the open window from the patio in the garden. The wafting scent of breakfast led him by his nose to the bacon and pastry.

Chaucer was the first to look up as Pinter joined them outside and it was difficult for Pinter to believe, with the freshness of his creased face, that he had been as drunk as a fish swimming in alcohol the last time he'd seen him. He smiled warmly: "Monsieur Rupert! I hope that you didn't sleep too uncomfortably?"

"I'll cope," Pinter mumbled, stretching his arms again before dropping onto the spare wicker chair that Chaucer had arranged around a well stocked breakfast platter. "You have a lovely home, Mr Chaucer."

"Christoph, please. Some coffee? Or tea? This is not England but I hope we can satisfy the taste buds nonetheless."

"A cup of tea would be wonderful."

"I hear you had quite the adventure last night, Christoph?" Randle chimed in between mouthfuls of a jam-lathered croissant.

"*Oui!* Had it not been for young Pinter here, I would have been in the...ahem...*merde*."

"Tres bien!" Randle laughed. "It would seem our Pinter is becoming quite the hero as of late."

"It would have been more heroic if the gun was loaded," Pinter said bluntly as he replaced the tea-cup on its saucer. Chaucer went white, and Randle laughed heartily.

"*Sacre bleu!* Geoffrey, you have with you a mad-man!"

Pinter couldn't help but laugh: "A mad-man that saved your arse from some rather nasty looking hoodlums."

"*C'est possible, oui.*"

"It's exactly what happened. You should be more careful with your debts...and with your debtors," Pinter replied in fluent French. Chaucer looked stunned for a moment, then suitably impressed. He slapped Pinter on the back:

"Excellent! Randle, I like this one!" He handed Pinter the toast tray and pulled out a silver cigarette case. Having lit a cigarette, he took a sip of orange juice and leant back in his chair, his face turning dark despite the beautiful weather. He drew on the cigarette and then exhaled a cloud of blue smoke slowly as he spoke: "While the company is a pleasure, gentlemen, I can't help but wonder what brings the two of you to my humble abode?"

Randle placed his empty mug of coffee on the table and leant forward conspiratorially: "The Spear of Lug."

Chaucer snorted as he refilled it: "A myth. Mere legend."

"If I thought you believed that we wouldn't be here. You've spent your life searching for it."

"And found nothing. Which is why I believe that it does not exist," Chaucer shrugged. "There is simply nothing to find, *mon ami*."

"That could all change."

Christoph suddenly became interested, leaning closer: "Go on?"

"We recovered the Dagda Cauldron a few weeks ago, and the Sword of Nuada was stolen from Theodore Marlowe a few days ago. You may have seen the news – the government are trying to make it an international incident. Claiming the Germans are behind it all. Nevertheless, the Stone of Fal vanished some time ago – presumably stolen. That's three of four found, Christoph. Which means perhaps you have a chance to redeem yourself in the academic community after all. Unless..."

"My God..." Chaucer cut in, twisting his cigarette between his fingers in anticipation.

"Exactly."

"The druids plan to resurrect the Tuatha De Danann? It can't be."

"It would seem so."

"Hold on," cut in Pinter, who had been quietly listening: "You're serious about this? Black magic, hocus-pocus? I know you said to have an open mind, but you're talking in serious terms about resurrection?"

"More than that," murmured Chaucer, darkly. "We're talking of the Otherworld, *mon ami*."

"The Otherworld?"

"Use your imagination, Rupert," Randle scolded. "What else would it be?"

"Silly question," Pinter conceded. "But what I don't understand is how getting through to the Otherworld will do them any good? It's a one way ticket."

"By resurrecting the Tuatha De, the world will be plunged into darkness," Randle began: "The Christian God will fall, Allah will burn...the religions of the world will be cast down and forgotten as a veil of darkness covers the world. The Tuatha De Danann were sorcerers...but they were insane. My fear is that even the druids don't have a clue what they're letting themselves in for." Randle's voice was grave. "Which is why we have to find the Spear before they do. Bringing the four treasures together means bringing together the four corners of the Earth. Four things that after the fall of the Tuatha De were never meant to touch again. With the power of those objects combined..."

"...chaos." Chaucer finished.

There was silence between them. Chaucer picked up a croissant and tore into it.

"What on Earth do they stand to gain from doing this?" Pinter said after a moment. "Surely this doesn't make sense, even to them?"

"They hope to gain enlightenment, I expect," Randle said slowly. "But it's what the Tuatha De Danann will resurrect as they come through from the beyond that will be the largest of our problems."

"And that would be?"

"The deities from whom they were descended. The stories vary, but we'd imagine Nuada himself will be among them. The God King of the Tuatha De, whose sword was the one Marlowe and his men retrieved from Turkey…to have it snatched away from under your noses."

"He whose sons are the Tuatha De Danann. If they're resurrected, they'll bring him back through from the Otherworld. That can only bring disaster." Chaucer's voice was grave.

Despite his skepticism, a ball of dread formed in the pit of Pinter's stomach. "I guess we'd better get going then. We haven't much time to lose."

"Christoph," Randle leant back, sipping his coffee. "Where does the trail start?"

"It took me thirty years and a considerable fortune, Dr Randle, but I can tell you not where the trail begins…but where it ends!"

"Which would be?"

"The *bibliotheque, mes amis!* Oxford Library!"

Pinter and Randle rolled their eyes at each other, but it was Pinter who vocalised their shared thought: "Right back where we started. We came all this way to go back home again."

"The clues are in the books my friends! But alas, I ran out of money and influence before I could complete the expedition. The pages we need are in the Caswell Collection, donated to the University in the late 19th century but kept out of sight, as per the request of James Caswell – the original owner of the collection. You need special permission from the head of faculty to even know where the books are kept, and as a disgraced academic I could not gain permission. Perhaps you two can!"

"I don't want to rain on your parade, Christoph, but I've been disgraced too."

"Ah," Chaucer's face dropped. "I see."

"I haven't," Pinter shrugged. "And the librarian owes me a favour or two. I'm sure we'll manage. What will the Caswell Collection tell us?"

Chaucer grinned: "The tomes will tell us where it was that the Order of St Francis hid the Spear when it came into his possession sometime around 1750-"

"I'm sorry," Pinter cut in: "The Order of St Francis?"

"*Oui*, Francis Dashwood."

"The Hellfire Club, Francis Dashwood?"

"*Oui*."

"You're certain?" Pinter asked sharply.

"*Bien sur.*"

"How was he involved in this?"

"This is something we will find out in Oxford University, young Rupert!"

Randle clapped his hands: "Excellent! Then we should leave at once!"

"*Oui!* I will pack my bag! I have waited almost 10 years, I cannot wait another second!"

Chaucer rose and rushed inside. For the first time Pinter was able to address Randle directly. "How far can we trust this man?"

"As far as we can." Randle's reply was clipped. The joviality he'd been addressing Chaucer with was gone – a very convincing act. Even Pinter was fooled into thinking Randle had an ounce of respect for the Frenchman.

"So you're saying we'll follow this madman into the gates of Hell?"

"If we need to."

Pinter shrugged and sat back, almost as though he were sulking: "I don't like it. And I don't trust him."

"You don't have a choice, Rupert. He could be our only hope in finding out what exactly is going on in this business."

Folding his arms, Pinter muttered: "That doesn't mean I have to like it."

Randle nodded, smiling as spoke: "True."

"Did he give any indication as to who ransacked the house?"

"He said he expected it was debt collectors. He's been able to lay low for long enough, but they're starting to catch up with him."

"It doesn't sit well with me."

"You're sounding more and more like your father," Randle smiled. "Do what he did. Trust me."

For a moment they sat in the glorious sunshine, noticing a storm moving rapidly from the coast towards them. The sun disappeared behind a cloud and all at once the wintry February air took hold of them. They'd been able to fool themselves for this long that it was a summer climate, but now a breeze began to kick and Randle rolled his eyes: "The problem with the Riviera. The weather changes at any moment."

Pinter grinned and took a sip of tea as a sudden chill caused goose bumps to rise on his arm. He had barely put the cup to his lips when the blood-curdling bellow rang out from within the cottage: *"Mon ami!"*

A gunshot echoed across the garden, and Pinter was able to catch the flash of light in the upstairs bedroom window.

Trouble, Pinter thought angrily: *This man is just surrounded by trouble.*

As he went for his holster, Pinter realised with horror that he'd left his revolver in the lounge.

From inside, he heard the voice of Chaucer yelling obscenities in French. The muffled sounds of a struggle followed, and then cold, calculating and almost hypnotic, the eerily familiar voice that spoke said firmly: "Please, calm down, Mr Chaucer. You're coming with us."

Pinter shot Randle a look and angrily muttered a word that turned the old man white. "Shakespeare."

EIGHTEEN

Pinter moved fast, ducking low and heading around the side of the cottage. Large hedgerows allowed him to stay out of sight of the windows. The clouds above now cast a dull grey light around him, and he felt the spit of the first raindrops graze his skin as he rounded the edge of the cottage and crouched behind one of the bushes near the gravel path for cover. There were only three men at the front of the house – at least as far as he could see. One was sitting in the car, puffing at a cigar and flipping through a magazine - presumably the getaway driver. Another sat in the back seat, a sub-machine gun resting on the open window and trained at the front of the house. He seemed bored, but his eyes darted from side to side, giving the impression that he was quite eager to use the gun at any appropriate opportunity. Pinter recognised the third man. Roach was leaning casually on the bonnet of their hired saloon with a white trilby pulled low over his eyes. A cigarette was hanging idly from his teeth, and he snapped a

Ronson lighter open and closed with frustration.

Pinter's hand instinctively went to his jaw, still bearing the pain of the brute force delivered by the big man's fist what felt like a lifetime ago. Conspicuously absent was Lawrence, who Pinter could only assume hadn't survived the encounter in the zeppelin. Though he felt guilty for being one of the men responsible for the thug's death, he couldn't help but feel relieved.

One less problem to deal with, really, Rupert thought to himself as he silently doubled back on himself. He gently pushed the door to kitchen ajar. The squeal of un-oiled hinges was audible, but only just, and with gritted teeth he crept through the house and into the sitting room. He could hear the sounds of a scuffle upstairs. Chaucer seemed to be packing a bag after all.

You bastard, Pinter cursed to himself. *You've sold us out already.*

His gun sat waiting for him in its holster atop the immaculate upright piano. The Webley was oiled, loaded and polished – the fruits of Pinter's labours the night before. The safety was still on, but it was a dilemma which he quickly corrected as he slipped his holster belt around his waist. He glanced out of the window. It appeared that the men outside weren't able to see him through the lace curtains.

The sound of footsteps on the stairs pricked his ears, and he brought himself up to full height. Whoever was using the stairs had to pass through the sitting room, so Pinter leveled the revolver and set his jaw.

I'm ready for you this time, Bill, he thought.

"You know, it's sad really," mused Shakespeare as he strolled casually down the stairs and into the room, his gun holstered and a cocky grin plastered on his face. "You're actually bloody predictable now, Pinter."

Pinter's fist tightened on the gun handle and his index finger brushed the trigger. This time, the gun was loaded. "Let him go."

Shakespeare laughed: "No."

It was as if the gates of hell themselves had suddenly opened, as from nowhere the windows exploded, sending shards of glass splintering into oblivion. Pinter leapt for cover and Shakespeare did the same, dragging Chaucer to the ground as the submachine gun outside tore the interior decor to shreds. The walls were pockmarked instantly and debris fell about them. As bullets struck the piano, a strange melody rang out, the snapping strings providing an even stranger percussion.

"Stop, you fools!" Shakespeare bellowed against the maelstrom. Just as suddenly as it had begun, all now fell silent. There was a moment where time itself seemed to stop. The last of the shrapnel from the destroyed sitting room settled on the damaged carpet. Pinter felt his heart in his mouth. Then, all too late, he realised that dropping his guard had given Shakespeare the upper hand. He found himself now crouched at gunpoint as his oppressor rose to his feet. Pinter could feel beads of sweat pooling on his brow, and despite himself, his hands shook. He couldn't think of anything smart to say, so instead slowly rose to his feet, his hands raised in surrender, and muttered to himself: "Bugger."

"This is becoming very entertaining," Shakespeare said sardonically. "I think this time I'll deliberately let you live. You make life so much more...fun." He dragged Chaucer outside, and for a terrible moment Pinter's eyes locked with those of the Frenchman. A mixture of both fear for his unfortunate position and relief that the gunfire had subsided. He considered that perhaps Chaucer was being taken against his will after all.

A clap of thunder echoed across the horizon and the heavens opened. The pathetic fallacy was overwhelming.

There was nothing for it. After all, he had nothing to lose. They had guns, but surely they wouldn't expect him to follow them armed only with a revolver? Perhaps they hadn't reloaded the machine gun? With adrenaline coursing through his veins, Pinter threw himself at the door, rushing outside with the gun in his hand to a sight that stopped his heart.

Geoffrey Randle realised immediately what a fool he'd been. The level headed caution of old age had been thrown to the wind when he'd heard the bullets spraying the house and in the pit of his stomach registered the danger his student was in.

It all came flooding back to him at once that for all intents and purposes Rupert was his charge – the only son of a good friend, and Alexander Pinter would be furious if he knew the danger the boy was in. How quickly he'd forgotten his paternal responsibilities when the chance for a treasure hunt came along.

No more. He'd flung himself from the wicker chair, the table toppling and sending croissants and toast flying, tea cups smashing as they hit the ground. But while his stamina for a man of his age was enviable among his colleagues and peers, his reflexes were not. He was no longer the youthful soldier of the Great War. No longer the marksman he had once been.

His hand was still on his holster as the first bullet seared through his chest.

The initial pain winded him, but he felt as though he could keep going. It was the bullet that tore through his shoulder and the bullet that sliced through his thigh that sent him falling headfirst onto the gravel driveway. The rain pelted down in full force. As he rolled onto his back, to feel the cold sting of rain against his cheeks one last time, everything seemed to slow down. It was as if the world was spinning more gently around the sun, or had stopped altogether for a moment. A horrible, cold sensation dragged his broken heart to the pit of his stomach as he heard Pinter shouting "No!" at the top of his voice. Then, through half closed eyes, the lids dropping in agony, he watched as the young man took off after the saloon that sped off into the heavy rain. He was too far behind to do any good rather than assuage his ego with the knowledge that at least he'd tried to do something.

Off they went, Chaucer with them.

Bugger, he thought to himself, as the pain flooded through him and he clutched hopelessly at the wound in his chest. *Randle, you bloody old fool. Look at what you've gone and done.*

Pinter didn't know what he stood to gain by chasing the car, but the fury that built up inside him drove him on as it crushed his chest and squeezed his heart. Fear held the tears back at first, but the surprising speed of the saloon stopped him in his tracks. For a moment he just stood, his arms hanging limply by his side. As the rain got heavier he wiped his eyes and turned back, too angry to watch the car vanish into the mist.

His mind flew back to Randle, and he ran as fast as he could to his professor's side, kneeling and cradling the old man. He'd lost too much blood, and it pooled around him, leaking from the wounds in his shoulder blade and chest.

Randle looked up at him, his eyes pained and full of death, but yet somehow kindly: "Too slow...and too old..."

"You'll be fine," Pinter lied, holding back tears as tightly as he could. His fists were clenched. "This isn't it. This can't be it."

"It is for me," Randle sighed heavily. Just talking now was painful. "Who'd have thought, eh? I survived the trenches, but I couldn't survive the French Riviera!" His joke fell on deaf ears, so he didn't pause for laughter: "You know, he warned me about that map. Old Tirey. Poor old Nicholas. He told me whoever touched it had signed a death sentence, and there he was the next morning...dead."

"Don't be foolish."

"I'm not," Randle chuckled. "I'm dying, aren't I? And I'll bet that those slimy buggers had something to do with it. Poor Tirey."

Pinter felt a tear force itself free of his grip and run down his cheek as the old man started to become cold. "What do I do now?"

"Stop asking questions and start making decisions, for a start. But above all, stop them."

"How, damnit?"

"Use your imagination, Rupert!" He coughed again, struggling to get words out at all now. But as he always did, Randle persevered, despite the agony that arched through his broken frame: "I didn't bring you along because you follow instructions. Get back to Oxford...find out where Francis Dashwood hid the Spear...and for God's sake..." he pulled Pinter in close: "...kick that bastard thug who shot me black and blue."

"Yes, sir."

"You're a good student Rupert. But for God's sake...transfer to history. Don't waste your degree on languages. Make me proud. I know your father would approve. He...he always did. Just didn't know...how to show it." Randle pulled him in close, his voice now a pained whisper as he clenched Pinter's collar to hold himself up: "A few words to live by, words that your father lived by too: if you must play the game, decide on three things at the start...the rules...stakes...and..."

Geoffrey Randle fell silent and went limp.

"...the quitting time." Pinter held him until he was gone, then carried him into the house as the heavy rain washed away the blood from the ground. His hands shook uncontrollably. He sat for a moment on the piano stool, his head in his hands, looking at the body through his fingers.

Randle was dead. His mentor. His friend – gone. As suddenly as that. Fear shot through him. Until now, he'd felt nearly indestructible, but this shook him to the very core.

But then, he thought, *that's what death does to you.*

He pulled a blanket over the old man, wiping away one last tear.

Untouched in a cabinet below the piano was a generous supply of liquor, and Pinter pulled out a decanter of whiskey and a glass. He poured himself a small helping and raised the glass in a toast to Randle.

I'll stop them, he told himself. *I'll stop them.*

Rupert Pinter took one more look back at the house, which now appeared oddly decrepit in the grey rain. It stood, he supposed, as a symbol of Chaucer himself – awash in grandeur until the facade fell away. He hadn't trusted the Frenchman from the moment he'd met him, and letting down his guard was what killed Randle.

Whether Chaucer was with them or against them didn't matter now anyway - Christoph had provided very helpful clues to carry on without him. The only fear that Pinter had now was how long it would take for Chaucer to change allegiances, if he hadn't already. For the right price, any man would sell his own mother, let alone his soul, even if it was to the devil himself.

He thought of Harry Lester. For a chap who appeared so interested in remaining mounted upon his moral high-horse, it hadn't taken much for his former peer to succumb to the temptations money and fame would bring. Perhaps Lester had even fancied himself as one of Shakespeare's gang.

If he'd made it that far.

He wound the engine and got into the Citroen. It was a tricky one to drive, but then he expected nothing less from a French car. There was a lot to do, and now more than ever, very little time to do it. As he pulled away from the home of Christoph Chaucer the world seemed suddenly to be an infinitely more dangerous place.

NINETEEN

Lana Marlowe closed her umbrella and shook the raindrops from it, stepping under the glistening canopy of the library foyer for shelter. The precious rock around her glittered as tracks of rain traced sparkling lines against the blue veins of the marble. The weather was horrendous and she had no desire to go back out into it.

The library was silent, lacking even hissing whispers that echoed through the wood panelled, marble-floored corridors. The typical sounds of the establishment were conspicuously absent. Her heels clicking on the cold stone floor alarmed her more than the mysterious sounds of night-time studying ever would. Even the rain seemed to have been silenced by the dead atmosphere of the place.

Lana knew Pinter well enough to know that when he was stressed or frustrated he retreated into the bowels of the library, disappearing into a sanctuary of worn, dust-bitten pages like a mouse burrowing into a hole for safety. If he was to be found anywhere in Oxford tonight, then this would be the place. The library closed only on Sunday nights, when the sound of the nearby Cathedral floated through the air and filled the empty halls, so the chances of him hiding away inside the literary confines on a weeknight was greater than his being resident at the flat he occupied a short walk away. It was either here that she would find him, or at the Daggers Club, but she had no real desire to go there. She wondered often what it was Pinter enjoyed about the ghastly place, but then realised that boys will be boys.

It was with surprise that when she did stumble across him he poring over a book with thick spectacles framing tired eyes in the Celtic History section; a wall of hefty tomes about him.

"I thought I'd find you here."

He jumped in surprise and looked up, warmth overwhelming his exhaustion: "Lana?"

"You didn't call. Or write, actually, it's been long enough for a postcard to have arrived. I was starting to worry that my father had said something that might have put you off."

He shook his head, trying to smile but failing miserably: "Nothing of the sort. I am sorry, though. I've been a bit busy for last few days."

"Oh, really?" The sarcasm was accompanied by her hands firmly slapping her hips.

"We went to the Riviera to find a man who could shed some more light on this whole business with Shakespeare. We found him, there was some trouble. Shakespeare appeared, as he tends to do. Randle died." He spoke bluntly. "I think the man who I fought in Wales on the expedition a few weeks ago shot him. A man called Roach."

She paused, shocked for a moment. Gently, she asked: "When?"

"Yesterday morning. I snuck aboard a train bound for

Calais then made my way back here. I've come straight here, haven't been home yet."

"Have you slept?"

"Not really. Not as much as I should have, at least. I managed a couple of hours on the boat and a few on the train. I'm alright."

She pulled up a chair and sat beside him, putting her arm around him as she did so: "Rupert, I'm so sorry."

"Me too." He took off his glasses and looked at her, deep into her eyes. Beyond the red-raw of fatigue, Lana saw a glimmer of hope in his: "Tirey was onto something, you know."

"What?"

"It's to do with the Sword of Nuada, as well as the artifact we recovered in Wales. Just as we thought."

"The Dagda...thing?"

"Cauldron, yes," he nodded.

"You've lost me already." She leant back in her chair and crossed her arms. "Rupert, what on earth are you talking about? I think you're right. You need to get a bit more sleep..."

"I think Shakespeare is some sort of mercenary. He has a good degree of historical knowledge too, which is why I'd imagine he's on hire to the Druids."

"The Druids? Don't be absurd."

He flushed: "It sounds ridiculous, I know. But all these things they're looking for are linked. They're all part of this myth about the 'Four Treasures'." He flipped open a book and turned it so that she could see it: "There were four colonies of myth, each of which held a magical object. They were the 'Four Corners of the Earth', so to speak, and from these islands came together the Tuatha De Danann – the earliest Druids. Magicians, maybe. But definitely occultists. Their influence in Celtic Britain and

Ireland was felt even by the invading Romans. The Roman chronicler Pliny wrote of them with distrust, clearly in fear of the legends that came with a land of gods and monsters and tales of demons that the Romans would have empathised with. Eventually they died out, persecuted by those who feared the new Christian God as the word of the Bible spread from the Holy Land to the rest of the ancient world."

His tone was academic, and Lana felt as though he was lecturing her. He quite often did it without realising, and she was certain that one day he'd make an excellent teacher.

If possibly a bit stuffy.

"What does all this mean, Pinter?" There was a spark in her eyes, as though she was angry he'd displayed more knowledge than her. Pinter grinned. She only ever used his surname when she was frustrated. "Well?"

"Four treasures. Four myths. Three proven true, and one left to find."

"Why find it?"

"The man we went to see in Monte Carlo, Christoph Chaucer, spent years studying this. He thinks they're using the treasures to resurrect the cult of the Tuatha De Danann."

"Which is where the druids come in?"

"Exactly. But I think we're in with a good chance considering what we're up against. Chaucer told me that the last of the four treasures, the Spear of Lug, was acquired by the Order of St Francis. In other words...the Hellfire Club."

She shrugged. "What could they possibly want with it?"

"Don't you remember your popular history Lana?"

"I'm a law student," she shrugged. "So no. Tell me?"

"They were notoriously ungodly. Pagan and ritualistic. Nasty pieces of work. It was basically an exclusive drinking club. Imagine the Daggers boys with a religious edge. Anyway, Francis Dashwood, who was the leader of the Hellfire Club, is supposed to have gotten his hands on the Spear sometime in 1790."

"So where did he leave it?" By now, Lana was entranced.

Pinter grinned boyishly, pulling out a dust bitten tome from the bottom of the pile: "His memoirs – part of a private collection. The library wouldn't acknowledge it existed until they realised I knew the name of it. Luckily, that means that there's no way Shakespeare could get his hands on it, and it also explains why Chaucer couldn't follow the trail as he didn't have access to it. Listen," he began to recite: "'And for the Spear by which the gods pierced the fabric of the world, that weapon which no target shall it ever miss, a chamber so deceitful in disguise to hide it was devised. For it was not our own machinations that provided the Temple of Lug, but the ancients themselves, whom we have honoured with protection beneath the Hellfire Temple, known only to minds of dead men forever.'"

"He must mean the caves in West Wycombe," Lana mused. "His private estate."

"I thought that as well, but it's too obvious. These were tricksters, notorious for their secrecy," Pinter said, shaking his head. "Which is why I checked this," he heaved another dusty book onto the desk. "A log of land purchase from the period. It's taken me hours to find it, but Dashwood owned a property in Scotland. A castle. If we find it, we'll be more than likely to find the 'Hellfire Temple' there."

Lana grinned broadly: "Well done, Rupert. Randle would be proud of you."

"I hope so. Either way, I'm leaving in the morning."

"Then I'm coming with you," she took his hand. "You should have the company at the moment."

Pinter sighed, then after a moment, said: "Are you sure? It'll be dangerous."

"I'm not letting you go running off and getting yourself killed. Besides," she deadpanned: "Who'd buy me dinner next week?"

He smiled: "Alright then."

"How very endearing." Bill Shakespeare's voice echoed around him as he stepped out of the shadows. "Quite the couple you two make. Pinter, you devil! You didn't tell me she was gorgeous. And a red-head too, you have good taste. Though personally I prefer brunettes."

"Shakespeare?"

"The very same. How wonderful we know each other's names, now, eh? Makes everything so much more...personable!"

Pinter went for his gun, but a flash of light stopped his right hand from moving any closer to his holster. He moved his hand back onto the desk, so that Shakespeare could see it.

"Ah, ah, ah," Shakespeare tutted as he waved his Luger around like a gunslinger in a western. He seemed to be enjoying every second of the action. "Up against the wall."

Pinter complied, taking Lana by the hand and moving them both slowly backwards until they bumped into the bookshelf behind them. With Lana sheltered slightly behind him, he spat back at Shakespeare venomously: "You won't get away with this, you bastard."

"Watch your language, this is a library, not a pub," Bill snapped, as he grabbed the book and tore out the relevant page. His smile was wicked as he did so. "Thank you for the notations, Pinter. I've no doubt at all that they will come in handy."

Pinter smiled back sarcastically: "My pleasure."

The smile turned into a deathly frown as Shakespeare

stepped forward and pressed the barrel of the gun into his chest. He could feel the cold steel digging into him and his heart beating against the bullet that lurked deep within.

They were close enough now that for the first time Pinter could look Shakespeare directly in the eyes. They were calculating, dark. Almost reptilian, like a snake measuring up its prey.

Bill reached out and pulled Lana to him, who struggled helplessly in his firm grasp as they stepped backwards.

Lana shot Pinter a look – desperation in her eyes. The gears in his mind whirred.

Oh no you don't, he thought. *Don't you dare.*

By now, Shakespeare had pulled Lana to the tall window that bathed the room in an eerie blue-purple light. He smiled.

"Cheerio!"

In one perfectly choreographed movement, he spun to face it, dragging a screaming Lana with him and to Pinter's horror he threw himself through the glass panes and into the storm raging outside.

TWENTY

By the time Pinter got to the window Shakespeare was already at street level two stories below him, dragging Lana roughly by the wrist towards a waiting parked car, the engine sidling as it lay hidden in the darkness. The zip-line attached to the window swung to and fro in the wind, whipping against the cracked panes of glass. Rain splashed into the chamber, soaking ancient manuscripts and destroying books. In another circumstance Pinter would have lamented the situation, but instead he lunged forward for the rope. Reaching for it, he was forced back to cover by a spark flying past his cheek as a bullet ricocheted off the stone wall beside him.

As quickly as he could, he pulled his gun-belt free from his waist and lashed it around the zip-line, pulling it taut and wrapping the ends he held around his fists. While it was horrifically unfashionable, he was immediately grateful for the fact that he was wearing braces to hold his trousers up. Pulling the belt close to him, he steeled himself, pulled his flat cap from his head and tucked it into his shirt, and then with a deep lungful of breath threw himself through the window. He swung perilously backwards as he descended the rope, colliding with the outside wall of the library about halfway down the zip-line. The complete lack of grace was accompanied by immediate danger as more bullets, spraying from the driver's seat of the saloon below, exploded around him and showered him with shards of splintered marble.

"Oh great!" He yelled to himself angrily. "What a fantastic idea this was!"

His instinct reaction was to let go, and the fall was mercifully brief. He crashed down onto the damp grass below with a painful thud, softened only by the knowledge that he was now sheltered by a thick hedgerow and the darkness. Pulling his hat out of his shirt and mashing it onto his head, he drew his revolver.

"Would it be too much to ask for just five minutes peace and quiet?" He moaned aloud as he checked the chamber, counting the bullets. "Just so I can get my breath back?"

The gunshots ceased, replaced by the screech of rubber on tarmac as the car took off from Ratcliffe Square and raced along Catte Street. Lana's screams were barely audible against the angry roar of the engine and the thunderous clap of rain. Pinter forced himself painfully to his feet and hopped over the hedge. The car was close, but he'd never catch it on foot. The cogs in his mind whirred uncontrollably and his eyes darted, looking for something that could prove useful in the pursuit.

Anything.

He allowed himself a cocky grin. Stood nearby was a glistening, brand new, British racing green BSA Blue Star. A beautiful motorcycle. He'd ridden once, maybe twice at a push thanks to the Dagger's Club, but he had a good grasp of how to handle the machine.

Besides, he considered, as he ran full pelt towards it, *I haven't got much of a choice.*

The lack of a helmet was an unfortunate evil, but one he could live with. There were more important things to worry about. The possibility of loaded weapons in the car he was chasing. He knew Shakespeare had a Luger, and the driver had a hand-gun of some description, but whether they still had the sub-machinegun with them was another matter. He swung his leg over the saddle and kicked the bike to life.

The 28 brake horse power engine roared in anxiety as it came to. The first maneuver was rocky as he pulled out onto the road and for a moment he thought he'd topple off straight away, but the bike went like a dream and within moments he was gaining more and more ground by the second as the rain slammed into his face. He tugged his cap low over his eyes. It would have to do as a helmet for the moment.

Shakespeare was the first to see the single headlamp appear behind them as they swerved onto Broad Street. He cursed violently before turning to Lana, his voice full of mock-pride: "Your boyfriend is full of surprises."

Her head spun backwards to take a look, and elation washed over the tone of her voice as she muttered back: "I'd say that you're in trouble now."

Shakespeare leant forward and tapped the driver on the shoulder, prompting Roach to grunt in acknowledgement as he gripped the wheel between thick fingers. The instruction from his employer was plainly put – clear and cold, blunt and cruel: "If he catches up with us, Mr Lestate, ram the young man off the road."

Roach nodded, and spun the wheel hard to the left, skidding into Turl Street.

Pinter was gaining ground comfortably when the first

bullet whizzed over his head, missing him only in the arc of his turn. It was, luckily, the only shot Shakespeare would make, as the other shadow in the back seat lunged at him and the two silhouettes struggled for the gun. Again the car turned, this time pitching dangerously close to the wall as Roach swung the automobile onto Ship Street.

Good old Lana, Pinter thought as he released the throttle to turn safely. *Maybe she'd be useful after all.*

It also meant his fears of the sub-machinegun were assuaged. He revved the engine and gained enough speed in doing so to bring him close to the car.

Close enough to lock eyes with Roach.

In the cold blackness of the thug's pupils, Pinter realised instantly that he'd made a terrible error in judgement. The excitement of catching up with them was gone. A sick feeling in his stomach stabbed at him as everything seemed to slow down.

The car pitched sideways towards him.

Here we go, he thought.

The crash of metal was deafening, and Pinter cursed under his breath as he realised he was being pushed towards the shop fronts lining the road.

He released the throttle again, dropping back far enough to let the car rush past. He immediately saw the danger he'd been in as the vehicle dashed against a wall, sending a shower of sparks into the air before spinning wildly left and onto Cornmarket Street.

Keeping his distance for a moment, his knuckles were white as he fought to keep control of the bike in the rain. He allowed another burst of untamed speed as they cut onto Market Street, drawing alongside with Shakespeare's car again as a row of oncoming parked automobiles loomed in the distance.

Again, Roach nudged to the right, catching the bike and

threatening to throw Pinter off, but while his leg ached with the impact he held firm, gritting his teeth through the pain.

The gap was closing with every second. His heart seemed to be racing faster than the vehicles. As he looked to his left, he saw Roach grinning venomously, his crooked teeth on vile display and his eyes alight with morbid amusement. He was clearly loving every moment of this. This was obviously an opportunity he'd been looking forward to since their skirmish in the mountains.

Carefully but quickly, Pinter reached out and made a grab for the car.

Roach realised too late, spinning the wheel in his hands and swerving to the other side of the road, which pulled Pinter along with them. The maneuver launched him off the motorcycle and he tumbled onto the roof, his shaking hands grasping the edge by their fingertips as his weight and the force of the turn threatened to roll him off the other side.

The bike spiralled out of control into an almost new, spotless Rolls Royce Phantom I, where upon collision it flipped, took flight, and burst into flames as it impacted with the roof of the car. It was a beautiful display.

From his new vantage point atop Shakespeare's car, Pinter watched the bike fall to pieces with a strange mixture of surprise, horror and huge relief.

"That was close," he said to no-one who could hear, trying to reassure himself that everything was going to be alright.

Heaving his weight to the driver's side, he swung his body against the window, smashing through and kicking Roach into the passenger seat in a single, fluid motion. The car swerved, now driverless and out of control, heading directly for a brick wall. Both Roach and Pinter grabbed at the wheel, steering the car out of harm's way and back onto Turl Street at the last second, before smiling at each other, pleased with themselves.

Pinter took even greater pleasure in landing a jaw shattering blow to Roach's grinning face, which sent the thug toppling out of the passenger door and onto the road behind them. He hit the ground rolling.

With the car now level, Pinter turned his attention to Shakespeare, who cowered in the back like a cornered animal. To his surprise, it was Lana who pushed Shakespeare out of the back door as they turned another corner, sending him bouncing along Broad Street. Pinter could only look on in reserved bemusement.

"Creep!" Lana shouted, her head hanging out of the open door. "And next time, watch where you put your hands!"

She huffed loudly, then pulled the Luger from where it had fallen by her feet. Throwing that out of the car as well, she slammed the door shut. The drama over, Lana looked up at Pinter and laughed — a mixture of relief and nervous tension: "You took your time!"

"I was pre-occupied. Strange escape route though, it would have been easier if he'd carried straight on. I wasn't sure how much petrol the bike would have." He paused for a moment, frowning: "We should go back, though. Bill has the map."

"No, he doesn't." Lana grinned and held up the pages Shakespeare had torn from the book, before clambering into the passenger seat next to him. "And it was terribly kind of them to leave us with a full tank of petrol."

Pinter laughed. "So you're coming with me, then?"

"Just try and stop me." She threw her arms around his neck and kissed him on the cheek, and he floored it, leaving rainy Oxford behind them in a gust of mist as the car took off out of town.

Shakespeare watched the lights of the car vanish into the distance. The fall had hurt like hell, but it was his ego above all else that was bruised. No permanent damage.

He pulled himself to his feet, and despite the rain smoothed the creases of his trousers. Roach ran up to join him: "I'm sorry, boss. Didn't see that one coming."

"I don't think either of us did. We haven't given that boy enough credit." He started walking towards his Luger, which lay on the road ahead. As he scooped it up, he looked longingly at it. "How very kind of them to give me back my gun."

"What do we do now, sir? They have the map. And the car!"

"Not to worry, Roach," Shakespeare murmured, transfixed on the dimming shadow of the vehicle as it became nothing but a speck on the inky horizon. "We'll catch up with them soon enough."

TWENTY-ONE

The rain had relented during the long, winding journey north. By the time Pinter and Lana had reached their destination – the towering, gothic Hellfire Castle, which stood perched precariously on the edge of a severe cliff - the storm had re-emerged with a vengeance. It brought with it howling winds and terrifying fingers of lightning that leapt down from the sky. The foul weather licked at the walls of the castle, and with every flash of blue light another section of the structure became clear. Towers that once reached to the gods had collapsed into the sea far below, leaving behind petrified, ruined stumps of cracked rock. In places, the castle itself had fallen apart completely, moss and vines claiming the ruins.

Pinter patted his flat cap onto his head and pulled his collar up tightly around his neck. The rain sent cold chills running down his spine. As he slung a shoulder bag onto his back, he drew his jacket near and muttered to himself: "I hate the rain."

"So do I." Lana was un-amused by the raging torrent whipping around them, and she too drew her grey trench coat against her, pulling the belt taut. "This isn't particularly romantic, Rupert."

"I hate to break it to you, but it was never intended to be," Pinter winked. "Come on."

They walked along the winding gravel road, wind and rain battering them without fathomable end. Pinter glanced back at the car, now beaten and severely weathered from their long journey. Oddly, it seemed almost sad to leave it behind. The grill appeared to frown as they walked further and further away. It struck Pinter that he might never see the car again.

Eventually, the shape of the castle grew prominent, silhouetted in the bleak light of the clouded moon. "There it is," Pinter nodded. "Hellfire Castle. It exists after all."

"A wasted journey if it didn't," Lana grumbled. "Dashwood must've had some money to spare."

"Seems that way."

The place was deserted. Curtains blew through broken windows and the wind howled in and out, creating a noise that sounded as if someone inside was screaming. Lana gripped Pinter's hand with all her might: "What did the old man at the Highland Crown tell you?"

As they'd made their way north through Scotland, Pinter had gathered that the old building was held in a sense of cautious awe. Barely anyone had acknowledged that it was there, but one old man with a weathered face and grave, ancient eyes had reluctantly imparted his sinister knowledge when they asked for directions at a local pub, fiddling with a ragged bow tie and a glass of scotch as he did so.

"He said this place is haunted. That it's been abandoned for centuries. The locals avoid it like the plague. They say that the men who built it were cursed to roam the corridors forever. There've been sightings...cloaked figures staring blankly out of windows at lost passers through. Childish ghost stories really. But a few years ago a group of researchers went in and never came out."

The words of the old Scotsman clung to the back of his mind: "And if you go in there, sonny...you'll not come out either."

Her face went white with fear and her grip began to turn his hand blue as she cut off the circulation. He gave her a warm, reassuring smile: "Don't worry. We'll be fine, trust me," he patted his revolver. "I came prepared. Besides, it can't have been abandoned for too long."

"Unless Dashwood inherited it...and never used it," she added, gravely.

He shrugged, squeezing her hand back. "Try not to think about it."

They reached the entrance, a colossal oak door firmly closed against nature. The iron hinges were rusted, but though he pushed the door with all his might Pinter couldn't open the thing.

"Guess I'll have to find another way around," he said to himself, but Lana scowled back at him, her eyes alight with determination that he wasn't going anywhere without her.

"And I'll just wait out here, shall I? What a brilliant idea."

He shrugged: "Maybe I can open it from the other side?"

She folded her arms and her scowl became more defined. "Don't be too long, or I'm going back to the car."

Pinter smiled, trying to break the tension: "I'll be right back. Don't worry. It's probably just bolted on the inside."

"And how exactly do you intend to get in?"

Pinter pointed at a window that hung open above them. "There."

"Good idea," she muttered sarcastically. "You're just going to jump up there then?"

"I'll climb the vines," he shrugged. "They look pretty strong."

Lana watched as he moved to the thick limbs that climbed the wall, and took a grasp of one. They were as thick as a strong rope, and he grinned weakly to himself, then turned to her and shot her a wink. She shrugged, unstirred.

I hope this works.

He moved cautiously upwards, hand over hand, not daring to look down. The vines held firm, though every creak as they strained under his weight made him wince in fear. Below him, Lana rolled her eyes: "You're not impressing me, y'know."

"Didn't intend to!" he called back. By now, he was close enough to the window ledge to reach out and grab it.

Nearly there.

He made a pass at it, pushing himself up as he stretched out his arm. His hand found its mark, and he pulled himself up further. The vines held firm. Tentatively, he climbed onto the window ledge, only looking back down when he was safely sat above.

"See! Nothing to it!" he called down. "I'll just find the stairs and be right with you."

Lana nodded, but didn't say anything, instead moving back to the door as Pinter swung his legs inside and jumped down to the floor.

His breath rushed from his lungs and he let out a sharp cry for help.

There was no floor.

He tumbled downwards in the darkness for a moment before landing on the sloping ruins of the upstairs floor, rolling as he collided with the ground and ending up crashing into the door of the room he was now in with a thud.

Around him was the dense scent of decay, an aroma of damp and rot, and beyond the thin shard of moonlight that cut through the door lay vivid darkness. Painfully, Pinter pulled a flashlight from his satchel and shone it through the doorway. The torch did little to help in the murky gloom.

At once, a figure moved before him, slowly approaching the door. He flicked the flashlight off and silently reached for his revolver.

His heart pounded against his chest. Surely they were just ghost stories?

His fingers were brushing the handle of the weapon as the door opened, and a voice called out: "There you are! The door was perfectly fine, you were just pushing it when you should have been pulling."

"Lana?"

"Who else would it be?" He could tell that she was rolling her eyes in the darkness. He flicked the flashlight back on and got to his feet, his joints aching.

"That was a silly idea."

"Are you hurt?"

"Maybe a little bit," he winced as he took a step forwards and a sharp pain raced across his ankle. *Not sprained*, he thought, *but pretty close.*

"It serves you right."

He reached her and adjusted his hat, moving the satchel comfortably back over his shoulder. Gently, he took Lana by the hand and pulled her with him, through the doorway into the corridor, and into the breach.

Beyond the door the howling of the wind was numbed into a low growl that echoed through the abandoned house. The faint light of the torch illuminated walls that had once been adorned with fine art. The paintings were degraded through years of atrophy, transforming expressive, elegant portraits into hellish images of the undead. Sunken eyes stared out from melting sockets, smiles twisted into grimaces. Whoever they were, they were a family of venerable Dorian Grays.

The hallways lay in ruin. Flooded corridors and mouldy carpets made traversing the mansion a difficult affair.

It struck Pinter immediately that there was only one route to follow: "Look at the flow of the water," he murmured. "It's going somewhere. Could be a dungeon, or catacomb, or something."

She nodded and they headed down the corridor, following the gentle trickle of the icy, murky water, clambering over debris and sections of the above floor that had collapsed after centuries of rot. Eventually the water flow pitched sideways and pooled at the entrance to a banqueting hall. Pinter swung the torch in for a look.

The hollow eyes of a decomposing skeleton stared callously back at him.

Caught off guard, he shivered a little, then forcefully halted Lana in her tracks and looked at her dead in the eyes: "Don't be scared. It's just a skeleton."

A squeal escaped her mouth as they stepped into the banqueting hall and Pinter realised his mistake. As well as the skeleton hanging near the door, the table was populated by feasting corpses, whose clothes, starched and rotten, held their bones in place in a ghostly tableaux. There was morbid comedy in the image, as the bird on which they were dining had decomposed as well. The whole picture was like one from a children's illustrated book.

"I think we were late for dinner," Pinter quipped, hoping for a nervous laugh from Lana – some sort of reassurance - but was met instead with wide eyes and terror. He took her hand and squeezed it tightly: "Come on. It must be through here."

Out of the corner of his eye, he noticed that the sheds of clothing on the skeleton with its back to the fireplace seemed caught in a gentle wind. He stopped dead, licked his finger, and felt the air. Nothing. The room was still.

"Look," he whispered, pointing at the cloth as it hung in the draught.

This time, Lana was quick to reply: "It's just a breeze from the chimney."

"Could be," he murmured, more to himself than to her. "But why is the cloth floating upwards, not downwards?"

He led her towards it.

The fireplace wasn't a fireplace at all. It was a stairway leading down.

Further into the darkness.

Despite himself, he shrugged.

Life is full of small fears.

Taking Lana by the hand, Pinter looked around the banqueting hall one more time. He was certain, almost certain, that the skeleton by the door had moved. Only fractionally, but noticeably different in positioning. Perhaps it was the way the arms were hanging...but surely the skull was facing the other direction when they'd entered?

He shook his head, guessing that it was just the shadows playing tricks with him. They were just ghost stories, after all, weren't they?

TWENTY-TWO

The stairs wound downwards into the bowels of the castle in a circular, anti-clockwise motion. Their movement was confined to shuffles as the tunnel became increasingly tighter and more claustrophobic. Moving forwards in single file and in complete silence, neither dared to speak as the darkness enveloped them further. The storm raging above their heads was hushed by their distance underground, becoming nothing more than a quiet hiss before it was gone completely. Their feet tapped against worn and damp rocks, mud squelching as they moved.

The path seemed to go on forever, into the underworld itself. Pinter shrugged off the dread that they may never see the surface again. To make matters worse, he couldn't help but wince as occasionally the squeak of a rodent pierced his ear drums.

Maybe this really is hell.

He adjusted his hat, allowing himself a little shiver before squeezing Lana's hand. He knew all too well that he had to be the strong one here, but even he was scared.

"Are you ok?" she whispered.

He nodded, though she couldn't see him. "I thought I heard a rat. I hate rats."

Eventually the winding stopped and the tunnel opened up before them. A spacious, looming cave, evidently painstakingly carved by hand beneath the castle. As he swung the torch from side to side he highlighted a line of cells that stretched out before them on either side. Pinter nodded to the piles of bones that had crumbled beside the cell doors: "I guess they're occupied."

Cobwebs hung like thick sheets from the floor to the ceiling about halfway through the cave ahead of them, and Lana shuddered at the sight. "Spiders. I'll bet huge spiders. Really, really big ones." Her voice trembled and she bit her bottom lip.

"Don't worry," he said gently. "They'll just be bigger versions of house spiders. Perfectly harmless." He swallowed, then under his breath and quietly enough for her not to hear, muttered: "I hope."

They stepped closer to the cobwebs and the danger that the simplistic and messy design presented became clear. The web was at least an inch thick and spread across the width of the dungeon.

"If we touch that, we're not going anywhere very fast. Unless the resident is hungry, I guess."

Lana looked up at him, her eyes flecked with a mixture of anger and fear: "So...what do we do? We can't turn back now."

Her voice was pleading that they did exactly that. Pinter nodded, absently surveying the room, looking for anything that could help.

Lana caught his grin out of the corner of her eye. "What?"

He stepped to the wall beside the door, pulling the archaic torch out of the socket. It was ancient iron with a wooden handle - sturdy and heavy - but he held it firmly and comfortably in one hand.

He moved purposefully to the nearest cell, reaching in through the metal bars and pulling some rags from a pile of bones. Balling them up at one end, he wrapped the rest around the top of the torch before dousing them with the contents of his hip flask.

Satisfied, he turned to Lana: "Terrible waste of gin. Hand me your lighter."

Even Pinter was surprised at the rate at which the cobweb wall burnt away, hissing and spitting as it singed down to a thin pile of ash at their feet. He led the way through, the burning torch now illuminating a great deal more than the flashlight. The detail of the dungeon revealed to them was morbid – locked cells empty apart from piles of bones; walls scratched frantically by fingernails, scarred by centuries of terror. The sight was gruesome, and Lana gripped his hand tightly. He supposed it was to stop her own from shaking so fiercely, so he squeezed back, turning to her and flashing a boyish smile. She smiled back, though her eyes were wide in fear.

"Don't worry," he whispered. "We're perfectly safe down here. They're just stories. Old wives tales, nothing to them really."

She nodded silently, and they kept going further into the darkness.

A low, pained howling that echoed through the dungeon stopped them dead in their tracks. He held the torch aloft, trying to illuminate further. Ahead of them, the tunnel seemed to close off and become more claustrophobic. Though the flickering orange light was strong, they still couldn't see particularly far.

"What the hell was that?" Lana shuddered, pulling Pinter to her and wrapping her arms around him. His own heart raced:

"I have no idea." His hand went instinctively to his Webley, patting the handle and unclipping his holster: "I'm glad I ended up bringing this."

He withdrew it and nodded forwards, to where the dungeon seemed to end and pitched downwards again, further into the darkness. "Whatever that thing was, it was down there. And there's only one way forward."

She shot him a look, and he cocked the gun, leveling it ahead of them.

"Come on."

They followed the tunnel downwards. The dread crept back as the walls closed in and they were forced to walk in single file again. Lana kept close, practically pressing herself against Pinter as he led the way.

After what felt like a mile of endless walking, they reached a rotting wooden doorway, which hung slightly open.

Looking down, Pinter saw what was keeping it ajar – the thin, decomposing skeletal fingers of a severed hand.

He swallowed deeply. This was becoming a bit much.

Gently, he pushed the door open.

The light cast into the room revealed a group of mutilated corpses, their faces locked forever in a look of pure terror. It appeared that they had been scrambling to safety, but somehow never made it. Oddly, there were no bloodstains, and no wounds on the bodies, which were still relatively fresh. A pair of cracked spectacles threw light into their eyes.

Lana covered her mouth to stop a scream escaping. Pinter shuddered.

"Looks like we found the research team."

Terror rocketed through Lana, freezing her to the spot. Fortunately, in its wake, the fear stopped her from being sick at the pitiful sight that lay before them. Pinter handed the torch to her and pulled out his flashlight, clicking it on as he crouched down to investigate the corpse further.

He had been a middle aged man when he had died. The look of strained, horrified fear that was forever to be his final death mask was disturbing. It struck Pinter that whatever this man had seen, or been killed by, was something perhaps not of this earth.

A piece of parchment hung conspicuously from the fingers of the inert researcher, and gently Pinter pulled it free, opening it up to reveal a crudely drawn map.

Or at least, what he assumed to be a map.

"Strange..." he murmured aloud, finally prompting Lana to become unstuck and step closer in interest.

"What?"

"This map," he said slowly, "looks more like a riddle to me. Frankly, its good luck for us that these chaps didn't make it out alive. Otherwise we'd be stuck. There isn't a floor plan, just a series of symbols."

"Lucky us," Lana muttered.

"If you look at it," Pinter continued, growing more excited with every syllable, "you'll see that they found something down here. Nobody knows what...not even them, I'd expect. But I imagine Dashwood wouldn't go to this much effort unless he had something important to hide."

"You think we were right then? That the Spear is here after all?"

"I'm almost certain. I found a parchment similar to this inside the Dagda Cauldron. It means we're on the right track." He swallowed deeply: "I just hope that we don't end up like these chaps."

A howling that echoed through the cave cut their self commendation short. Lana shivered and Pinter raised himself to full height, pocketing the flashlight and grabbing the torch. His hand went again to his revolver. "Come on, we've got to hurry."

He hastily passed her the map, this time not trying to disguise his own fear.

"You navigate."

They moved quickly, passing through the room where the collection of corpses lay in agony for eternity, and down a passage that led to a turnpike. This section of the catacomb was remarkably different – more crudely carved into the walls and much older, it seemed, than the chambers they'd already passed through. They now had two choices, and scanning the arched faux marble doorways, Pinter noticed familiar imagery.

"Rising sun or waxing moon?" He blurted.

"I beg your pardon?"

"On the map. Do we follow the rising sun or the waxing moon?"

A painfully long pause gave the sweat on his brow a moment to roll to his chin. Then finally: "Waxing moon...I think."

"The symbols lead the way. Genius!" Pinter couldn't help grinning despite the rising panic. "I wonder where they found the map?"

"Come on!" Lana pulled him with her as the chaotic howling drew closer, the echoes louder.

They were running now, the tunnel straight-forward and wide enough for them to run side by side, but wet with condensation. The walls dripped with mud, which in the light of the torch looked like thick blood running down the sides of the passage. Again, they came to a junction and over Lana's shoulder, Pinter frantically looked for the appropriate symbol to lead their way. She was switched on now, taking him by the hand and leading him down a passage marked by a full moon. This passage twisted and turned, but before long they'd reached another junction.

"Rising sun!" Lana called before they'd even stopped running. They ducked into the next tunnel and kept going. The howling seemed closer than ever now, and Pinter could almost feel hot breath on their necks, as they reached the next junction.

"Noon sun!"

They ran for their lives, and found to their horror that it was a dead end.

Aw Christ, Pinter thought.

He shot Lana a scared look: "Damn. Do you think we took a wrong turn?"

"The symbol was pretty hard to get wrong."

"Great." He adjusted his collar in the sudden heat, sweat starting to pour from his brow onto his temples and pool where his flat peak cap met his forehead.

It was too hot.

Despite the fact that they'd been running, it was far too hot.

Something struck him as strange and he watched for a moment as their shadows danced frantically on the wall in the light from their burning torch.

"This doesn't make sense," he murmured. Then it struck him, and he grinned. "This door is a fake."

"Huh?"

"The air is being sucked through. Look at the way our shadows are moving...they're dancing and we aren't. There must be a lever or something. A fulcrum release that opens the door."

He spied it – a symbol on the door in the shape of

concentric circles. Pushing it as hard as he could, he felt the earth shudder as gears turned and cracked. Slowly, with a plume of dust, the door opened, revealing on the other side a huge, imposing temple, at the heart of which sat the spear. It reminded Pinter of the chamber which had housed the Dagda Cauldron. Heat rushed out at them, created by the eternal fires burning within that encircled the chamber.

Perhaps, thought Pinter, as the hot wind tried to steal his hat and he pressed it tightly to his head, *we've found hell after all.*

"Incredible," Lana whispered.

Pinter nodded, stepping over the threshold and pulling Lana with him.

The door slammed closed behind them, saving them from the vicious noises bearing down on them but sealing them inside in the process.

The lesser of two evils, he figured.

Pinter turned to Lana and shrugged: "Out of the frying pan…"

TWENTY-THREE

It was only a split second after the huge stone door had crashed closed that Pinter's blood ran cold and he felt sick to his stomach: "Oh...I had wondered."

Lana shot him a look: "What now?"

He nodded to the swarm of furry creatures chewing a roasting corpse, boiling from years of slow cooking by the heat of the chamber: "Rats. I really, really don't like rats."

She gave him a sarcastic look: "You're kidding me, aren't you? Rats? Some people keep them as pets for crying out loud!"

"No, I'm not joking." He shuddered at the sight of the rodents scrambling over the dead body, bloated and grilled to a near crisp. The click of claws and the tearing of skin as the rats clambered over the decimated face of what had once been a man disgusted him to the core. "I should've thought it was strange that there were none along the way. They were all here for the free meal."

Lana took his hand slowly, pulling him out of the

horrified trance: "Come on. We're close now."

They skirted round the pile of vermin and got closer to the Spear, which at sat atop a pedestal inscribed with Celtic carvings. Pinter crouched down to investigate, closing his ears to the sound of his nearby phobia.

His eyes opened wide with surprise: "Latin? There's Latin here?"

"How?"

"Must be something to do with Dashwood and his cronies. I think I can read it. It's scratched in so it's been here less time than the Celtic symbols. 'May he who disturbs the Spear from its slumber anger the eyes of the Gods themselves.'"

Lana shrugged as he looked up at her, and his eyes moved quickly to the wall behind her. "What could that mean?" she murmured, and then, almost to herself: "When did you learn fluent Latin? I'm a law student and don't know that much."

"I went to a grammar school. I didn't really have a choice. But that's beside the point."

He pointed to the murals that were carved into the wall – fierce images of Pagan and Latin gods locked in unearthly combat. An almost sexual overtone to the nudity struck him as a product of the Hellfire Club, but the money and design invested in this all was beyond imagination. He could only assume the divine imagery had been damaged by the members of Hellfire when they discovered the cavern.

"I reckon Dashwood and his cronies discovered this temple and built the dungeons and the castle on top of it. It must have been centuries old when they found it."

"How can you tell?"

The hollow eyes of the carvings filled him with dread: "I think it's a trap. Look at the wall. Only the Celtic gods have hollow eyes, and they seem to be spaced evenly apart.

Yeah…it's some sort of trap."

"Sounds about right."

"Always does in places like this."

"Well…" Lana sighed. "We came all this far. How bad could it be?"

"Use your imagination," Pinter deadpanned.

"Good point."

He crouched for a moment, staring at the pedestal and stroking his chin.

"How heavy do you think that thing is?" He mused aloud, indirectly towards Lana as he considered the Spear. If this trap was similar to the one in Wales, perhaps it was a case of replacing the weight. If it matched, maybe whatever would be unleashed upon them would never come to be.

"Not sure. It looks like it's just a large arrow head, really. Probably about the same as your hip-flask when it's full."

Pinter sighed, took off his cap and scratched his head. "Typical. That hip flask was my father's. And it's empty, anyway."

Lana, to his dismay, handed him a canister of water: "Not anymore!"

"Thanks," he muttered, allowing a moment for his sarcasm to register properly. "Why don't we just use the canteen?"

"Too heavy, Roop. Just use the hip flask. You can't hold onto these things forever."

He grumbled inaudibly to himself as he filled up the hip flask with water from the canteen, then handed the canister back to Lana and stepped to the pedestal. He weighed the hip flask in his hand. Over his shoulder, he shouted: "I hope this works."

His eyes met those of the gods on the temple wall and a trickle of sweat traced down the goose-bumps of fear on his neck. He shuddered.

It was now or never. And he was far too close to just give up.

His hands shook as he lined up the switch.

Close. Too close. Lana stood wide eyed behind him.

"Sorry, dad," he whispered.

In a swift, careful movement, he switched the objects, picking up a piece of parchment that sat beneath the Spear as he did so.

There was a horribly long silence.

Nothing happened for a few, blissful moments. He dared not breathe, instead staring at the hip flask resting on the pedestal, willing it not to move.

Willing hell to remain leashed.

Pinter ran the Spear of Lugh between his fingers. Just as the Dagda Cauldron had done, it sent a tingling sensation through him, a sensation that even in the intense heat of the chamber was conspicuously warm and inviting. Slowly, and with a degree of trepidation, a wave of success rolled over him. He exhaled heavily and without thinking he wrapped the Spear in the parchment.

It was only once he'd stepped back to Lana with the prize clutched firmly in his hand that he felt the tremors. She went white. The ground shook beneath their feet, and he heard a crushing rumble echoing from the nothingness. The rats, no longer preoccupied with the feast at their feet, began piling over each other in panic, scrambling towards a way out. Some scattered across the chamber, while others, drunk on the food and heat, ran straight into the fire that circled the chamber and were killed instantly.

As the trembling grew in intensity, Pinter had to steady himself, placing the Spear in his bag and taking the torch from Lana.

"Maybe one day I'll get it right!" He moaned as grabbed her by the hand and pulled her back to the door. As with the other side, a pressure pad sat in the centre of the rock. He heaved his body against it and the entrance rose slowly. A low hissing noise pricked his ears.

His eyes automatically snapped to meet those of the gods. Green smoke billowed out of their hollow gazes. He held his breath and, dropping the torch, clasped his hand over Lana's mouth and nose, giving her a stern 'Don't breathe' look. She nodded, brushed his hand away and clamped her own palm in its place.

Then, without warning, the gas burst into flames.

And started growing into a column of fire.

Pinter's eyes went wide as he realised that the moment the gas touched the flames circling the chamber, it combusted. The trap wasn't the gas - it was the flamethrower. Or flamethrowers, as around the chamber the eyes all began to flame with contempt.

Moving quickly, he snatched up the torch again pushed Lana out of the chamber, crawling through the space that had opened up beneath the door. They were through the doorway and clear by the time the roof of the cavern was engulfed in a bright cloud of hell-fire. Pinter took a last look back at the rats, as they writhed in pain, scattering to escape the fire and twisting and turning in a horrific dance of death.

He couldn't help but feel slightly relieved.

The huge stone door slammed shut behind them, sealing the flaming temple away forever, and his beloved hip flask with it. Pinter and Lana both sucked in relatively fresh air, pleased more than anything to be alive.

Looking up, Pinter was the first to see the cloaked figures looming before them, their faces covered by black hoods. Whoever they were, they didn't seem friendly, and were approaching fast in the claustrophobic confinement of the passage.

"Wonderful," he muttered, as he rose to his feet, readying himself for the confrontation. "It never ends, does it?"

TWENTY-FOUR

The revolver was in his hand and the trigger depressed as an instinct reaction. The chamber hissed and a bullet rocketed from the barrel of the Webley, coursing through the shoulder of their nearest attacker with a sickening crack of splintering bone.

Pinter dropped the torch and took Lana by the hand, barging past the cloaked, wounded figure as the others scattered at the sound of gunfire. Thin, skeletal fingers grabbed at them but they were moving too fast now for the feeble attempts of the creatures to stop them. As they ran, chaotic howling transformed into moaning pain as streaked blood trickled down the walls of the tunnel. Nothingness enveloped them as they ran, and though their eyes were slowly becoming accustomed to the dark, it was still viciously opaque all around them.

Pinter held Lana tight and dragged her back through the passage, back towards the dungeon. Back towards safety.

Or so he hoped. They were barely out of the labyrinth

when they felt the hot, foul breath of the nearest cloaked...*thing*...on their necks. The creatures were gaining, and they were bloody fast. He was grateful they'd had it easier getting out than in, but knew full well that they couldn't run forever. Sooner or later those things were going to catch up with them, and when they did...

Don't think about it, he told himself angrily. *Just think about getting out.*

Up ahead was the wooden doorway and Pinter let his mind step up a gear. If he could close the door between them and the cloaks then it would buy them some time.

Not much, but enough to get back to the car and out of sight and sound of the monsters following them.

It all made perfect sense, all seemed so simple. Deep down, he knew it was never going to be that easy, but he let a cocky smile cross his face.

"Come on!" He yelled to Lana, over the ferocious howling around them. "Almost there!"

She looked up at him in terror, tears of fear running down her cheeks: "What?"

"The door!"

She nodded, and they tore past the corpse that lay in the way. They were aware now of what it was that had frozen its face in terror.

The former researcher was a ghastly omen of their possible fates.

Pinter kicked the rotting hand away from the door frame and with Lana safe in the dungeon, he slammed the door shut and pulled down the wooden slab that acted as a lock. The wood was rotting but held firm, and as the crash of wood on rusty hinges died away, an eerie silence fell. Pinter breathed heavily, wiping sweat from his brow.

Lana's whisper trembled: "Are we safe?"

Pinter held his breath, not daring to speak. The room

was desperately dark now that they hadn't got the torch. He pulled the flashlight out of his pocket and flicked it on, spotting Lana sat against the wall, trying to light a cigarette with her Ronson. Her hands were shaking too much to work the thing, so as he collapsed against the door, sliding down to take a seat, he took it from her.

"I hope so," he murmured. "This isn't the time, Lana."

"I can't light it anyway."

"Good. It's a bad habit."

"It's not like you've never done it," she grumbled.

"I don't make a fashion of it. Anyway…"

The argument was cut short by the crash of fists against wood. The ferocity was unbelievable and Pinter was back on his feet before the second barrage. He stumbled back towards Lana, tripping over debris on the floor. Looking up at the ceiling, he shouted skyward to Randle's ghost again: "Just two minutes rest, is that too much to ask?"

"With you," she said slowly, relishing a light moment in the abhorrent situation: "A couple of seconds would be far too much to ask for."

"I'm glad you agree."

He took her hand and they rushed back towards the winding staircase, taking two steps at a time. Behind them, they heard the rusted hinges buckle and snap. A crash echoed up the passage as the wooden door exploded and splintered below. Frenzied footsteps were gaining ground far too quickly for comfort. With Lana in front of him up the stairs, Pinter found himself pushing her, willing her on, all the while looking back over his shoulder with one hand resting on his gun holster. They stumbled, but fear drove them forwards, winding skywards dizzyingly quickly.

After what seemed like a lifetime, they burst out into the banqueting hall, but to his horror, Pinter saw that they were not alone.

More of the hooded creatures occupied the house. In the pale light of the cloud-caught moon he could see horrific skeletal masks beneath their cowls. Deep-set eyes in sunken grey skin met his gaze. If the creatures were ever human, it had been a long time since they'd had even the slightest semblance of humanity.

They were repulsive. That was for certain.

To make matters worse, they had formed a circle around them. The others appeared from the stairwell.

Lana threw her arms around Pinter, burying her head in his chest, whimpering helplessly.

With his gun in one hand and his free arm around the girl, Pinter faced down the biggest of them, his eyes darting between them all.

He leveled his Webley at the head of the leader, sweat dripping from his brow as he faced black, empty, hopeless eyes.

There was no way out. This was it.

His hand shook, and he tried not to look at Lana. Her fingers were gripping his shirt harder and harder as the wave of panic crashed through her. He felt his arm tightening around her too, pulling her close.

Oddly, despite it all, above everything else he could smell her coconut-scented red hair. It was reassuring against all the odds.

"Ah, shit..." he muttered, his finger tightening on the trigger.

Then, suddenly the figure buckled over in terminal anguish as a bullet ripped through what was left of its heart.

In a panic, the others turned to flee in a rush of black cloth, sweeping around them, out of the way, and vanishing back to the stairwell. As they parted, Pinter was able to make out the crowd of people in the doorway, who now began switching on flashlights and swinging rifles back over their shoulders.

"Bully!" A familiar voice boomed jovially. "What an excellent shot, eh, Pinter? And just in time!"

TWENTY-FIVE

Shakespeare stepped towards them as the cloaked figures moved slowly back towards the fireplace. He was casually swinging his smoking Luger from his fingertip as he did so. Pinter noticed that just as he had been in Wales, Shakespeare was now dressed rather flamboyantly in a tan colonial hunting suit, the braces attached to his high-waist trousers hanging limply around his hips. His khaki jacket hung casually about his shoulders as if the man were off to watch a few overs at Lords. Even in the dull light of the moon his freshly polished boots glistened spectacularly. It struck him that he may never see Shakespeare with even a speck of dirt about him.

Pinter holstered his own gun and sighed angrily, looking at the floor like a reprimanded schoolchild: "Damn."

"That was a lucky escape." Shakespeare's voice had an almost sing-song quality to it as the creatures shrank away in the glare of yet more lights that were approaching from the connecting hallway. Pinter couldn't help but admire the man, despite despising him.

"You took your time, Bill. I was expecting you to be waiting in the chamber for me this time," Pinter spat, looking the man directly in the eyes now. "At least you bothered to turn up at an appropriate moment."

"You will have noticed that I have a talent...no, a *penchant*, for creating an entrance," Shakespeare smirked, as his collection of heavily armed, torch-bearing thugs moved forwards, surrounding them. Pinter wasn't sure which was worse – the creatures or these fellows. "I trust that you have the Spear, Pinter?"

"You know full well that I do."

"I knew full well that you wouldn't let me down! Chaucer and I had every faith in you."

Pinter spotted the Frenchman cowering behind Roach. They were both stood near the doorway, but Roach came closer, grinning sadistically. Rupert looked over Roach's shoulder: "Hello again, Christoph. I take it you've changed sides, then?"

"I'm sorry, Rupert...but the money! It was too much to deny, *mon ami*. Particularly the way things are, you must understand..." Chaucer's voice trembled.

Pinter felt the resentment bubbling inside him. His tone became more aggressive: "I'm just sorry that Geoffrey Randle was wrong about you. He thought you had integrity. Maybe that was his fatal mistake."

Chaucer flushed with embarrassment and Pinter turned his attention back to Shakespeare: "What were those things?"

"They're called the 'Guardians' by some. Local ghost stories. More likely just insane, bastardized Druids...the ones left behind," he replied, his tone muted and for once deadly serious. "Who knows? Scary stuff, though, eh? And to think that they were chasing you! Good thing we turned up in time, what?"

"I suppose so."

"I'd like the Spear now, please. I don't want to use the gun, but I will if I have to."

"You can try," Pinter muttered just loud enough for his adversary to hear but for the sentiment to be inaudible to the armed mercenaries nearby.

"Don't be blind, old boy. There's no other way out of here," Shakespeare said simply. "Hand it over, Pinter, and save yourself the hassle."

Begrudgingly, Pinter reached into his bag and withdrew the Spear. He could feel the hairs on the back of his hand rise as he touched the treasure, the almost electric energy rushing through his fingers. He looked at Lana with an expression that told her he was sorry. Her eyes begged him not to, but he reluctantly handed it over to Shakespeare.

"You're meddling with powers way beyond your control, Bill. I hope you know what you're doing."

"I'm not the one meddling, Rupert. You can give credit for that to my employers."

"So...what now?" Pinter asked limply. "Are you going to kill us anyway?"

"Goodness, no! Nothing so brash. I'd rather keep an eye on you for a bit than have you running off and getting yourselves into trouble again."

"I'm sure you would."

"For such a smart chap, you can be terribly stupid," Shakespeare muttered, apparently displeased. Pinter snorted, almost laughing, until his opponent murmured a word that caught the laugh in his throat: "Roach?"

The brutish thug stepped forward, and Pinter knew him immediately as the man who had not only given him a good going over in Wales but now, and more importantly, as the man who'd killed Geoffrey Randle.

His blood boiled. Somehow, despite the fire coursing through his veins, he managed to maintain a modicum of control, looking up at the broken nose and smirking. It was a cocky, arrogant, and very dangerous smile: "Hello. Long time no see."

Roach laughed. It was a deep, unsettling noise. One that chilled Pinter to his very core. That familiar sense of dread that seemed to connect the two returned as he heard a knuckle crack out of sight. Then another. Then the whole fist.

He swallowed deeply, then tried to smile again: "Sorry about your nose."

Roach shrugged, and for a moment relief washed through him. Maybe he'd escaped a beating this time.

There was a wonderful moment that followed. It seemed to happen when the meaty fist launched without warning, or any indication, into his skull. The sudden motion sent his world spinning. Pinter couldn't help but feel that perhaps he'd pre-empted the situation appropriately with his instinct reaction of terrible fear. It was proof, at least, that his instincts were right, even as a terrific pain ripped through him.

He watched the room dance, observing the swirls of colour as they became an enchanting blur.

What a fantastic right hook, he heard himself think deliriously.

Then there was nothing at all but a comforting, numbing blackness that wrapped around him like a blanket. He let the nothingness claim him, and the last thing he felt was his frame slumping heavily to the floor as his cap leapt from his head.

TWENTY-SIX

A shaft of light cut through the blurred opaque surroundings like a sharp blade through straw. Pinter stirred in time for a pair of thick-fingered hands to drag him out of the car trunk and dump him onto the dirt floor outside. The world spun as it had the last time he'd been able to remember and his head throbbed uncontrollably.

How long have I been out?

One of his teeth wobbled as he lifted a hand to rub his jaw, and he tasted iron as blood wept onto his swollen tongue.

At first he felt as though he'd never speak again, but with a sandpaper throat he managed to cough at the blurry, heavy set figure stood above him: "We're here then? Finally! Hardly what I'd call first class travel."

As his vision returned, the first thing he registered was that they weren't in Scotland anymore. The sun shone brightly and it was as if it had never rained at all. Even in as bleak a position as this, Pinter couldn't help but smile. No more rain, and no more rats, either.

Today was shaping up to be considerably better than the last one that he could recall.

He blinked heavily, rubbing his eyes as everything started to form shapes. His cap dropped to the floor beside him. Tentatively he moved towards it, still not quite sure how much feeling he'd be able to achieve in his limbs. His arms and legs felt numb, but he forced himself to reach over and place a hand on the reassuring texture of his hat. As he scooped it up and crushed it onto his head, he hoisted himself to his knees and took a proper look around.

They were at a campsite in the middle of nowhere, mountains in the far distance surrounding them. Tents lined his view, and the site seemed weathered, as if it had been occupied for while.

How long have I actually been out for? He wondered again, more desperate this time. *It must've been a couple of days.*

It was fairly warm, particularly for the time of year, and Pinter guessed that they were somewhere in the south-west. Which put them either back in Wales, to which he shuddered at the thought, or the south of England.

Maybe Cornwall. He hoped so - he liked Cornwall and knew a few chaps in Falmouth who may be able to help them out of this mess.

Them.

Lana.

But where on earth was she, if she was even here?

He watched Shakespeare emerge from one of the tents, his face a picture of colonial joviality, as if he'd slaughtered an African tribe before high tea. His suit was starched and fresh, though the dirt on his trousers and boots suggested that Bill had been getting his hands dirty. Pinter smiled to himself.

I guess he has to do his own dirty work sometimes after all.

They clocked each other immediately, and the heavy-set thug who'd assisted Pinter out of the car picked him up and pushed him vigorously towards his nemesis. He didn't manage to get a glimpse of the man's face, but could only assume it was Roach.

"You're awake!" Shakespeare called over, happily. "It's about time. Come on in, please join me for breakfast! You haven't eaten in days!" He motioned inside the tent.

Pinter was suddenly aware of the growing hunger in the pit of his stomach, and though his best judgment suggested that he decline the invitation politely, not knowing when the next chance for food would arrive put words into his mouth: "Sounds lovely. You fellows seem to have been quite busy without me."

Shakespeare shrugged: "My men are well paid and well prepared. If humble lodgings are necessary...lodgings that need to be disposed of quickly...then they are the best men for the job. The very best."

"I can imagine," Pinter spoke more steadily now, his voice returning and the feeling returning to his arms and legs. "I have to admit that I'm curious. Where exactly are you getting your funding from, Shakespeare?"

"The men are under the employ of my employers, to tell you the truth," Shakespeare replied nonchalantly as he led Pinter into the spacious tent and motioned for him to take a seat at the well-stocked breakfast table. "They work for me because their bank roll is exceptionally good. I can vouch for how good it is, in fact. Roach, on the other hand..." he motioned then to burly thug who leant against the tent pole, watching Pinter as he sat down: "...is a loyal companion of sorts. We've known each other for quite a long time. We worked together in the colonies for quite a while...after Oxford University and I decided we weren't quite right for each other, that is."

"He has a good right hook," Pinter deadpanned. Shakespeare laughed, and to his surprise, Roach grinned.

"He does indeed," Shakespeare said after a time, sinking into a deck chair opposite his guest. "Tea? It's Earl Grey. Excellent and the real business. You've been out for a couple of days so it will do you some good."

"That long? He really does have a good punch on him if you're not prepared for it..." Pinter shuddered at the thought of another beating and accepted a slice of toast, resolving to be on his best behaviour.

Besides, who knew where manners could get him?

He sat back in his chair and chewed it thoughtfully for a moment before asking bluntly: "Where is Lana?"

"She happens to be in first class accommodation. I'm sorry that you had to spend your time in the boot of the car. It just seemed to make sense. You'll be happy to know it's the same car you stole from me in Oxford. There's a fair amount of mileage on her but you took good care of her, much obliged! As for the girl, she's fine. Don't worry."

"Then forgive me if I do worry. I want to see her."

Shakespeare smiled and lifted the teapot in front of him: "All in good time, old man. We have plenty to discuss first. Pressing matters at hand. Most importantly – how do you drink your Earl Grey?"

"No milk, no sugar, just a slice of lemon if you have it."

"A man after my own heart. Very few people know how to drink Earl Grey properly. In fact I was once entwined with a girl who positively drowned the bag in milk and laced the cup with sugar as if it was going out of fashion to do so," Shakespeare smiled as he dropped a slice of lemon into the cup and handed it to him: "But I'm digressing. Help yourself, the pot is full. There's plenty of fresh fruit and some of the breads are wonderful. Mr Chaucer brought them from France."

"I hope you'll understand if I decline the breads, then."

"Naturally. If I were in your position I think I should dislike Christoph just as much as you. In fact, I can't say I'm a huge fan myself, but these affairs strange bedfellows make, as they say."

"I dislike, and I distrust."

"He's hardly a man of principles," Shakespeare conceded as he tore at a croissant. "Please, eat! Be my guest. Chivalry dictates that while we may well be opponents in this clash, as you are a guest in my house you must be treated as such. I'm a fervent follower of the school of gentlemanly capitalism, and it's frankly a pleasure to finally have a chance to chat to you beyond the confines of dangerous situations. Without guns, I mean."

Pinter nodded and bit a chunk out of an apple. "I know what you mean. You have quite flamboyant tastes, Bill. No offence intended, of course."

"Of course." He nodded, seeming to accept the comment as a compliment more than anything else, then sat back in his chair with a cup of tea in his hands and fell silent. His eyes moved over Pinter with a great degree of detail, as if weighing up every element of his guest.

The atmosphere was surreal, and Pinter had to stop himself from laughing out loud at how bizarre the whole affair was. Eventually, and at the point where the lengthy silence was bordering on becoming uncomfortable, Pinter swallowed another chunk of apple and leant forward in his chair.

"I expect you're waiting for the big revelation, where you can tell me the whole plan? Well…I can't help but wonder what the big picture is, Bill. What exactly is your game? You've done nothing but move in the shadows, and the moment I think I've got you pegged you invite me for breakfast. Who are you?"

"I'm a mercenary of sorts. The men I'm working for are paying me very well for what I'm doing, and frankly, while you are a thorn in my side of the highest degree, you are proving bloody useful. Invaluable, I'd say."

"Thanks."

"You're welcome. I won't mince words, because I imagine you've already come to a few conclusions, so I'll tell you outright that I'm working for the Druids. Or a form of them anyway. They want the Four Treasures of the Tuatha De Danann to resurrect the ancient sect and learn the deepest secrets of black magic. Beyond that, I have no knowledge or interest in what the devil they have planned. As long as I get paid, I don't give a damn. It's all quite simple really."

"It's insane. Completely barmy and utterly mad as far as I'm concerned." Pinter smiled.

"You don't believe?"

"I didn't say that. I'm just of a steadfast opinion that we shouldn't mess with the divine. But in my opinion, this Tuatha De Danann business is the stuff of nonsense. Superstitious hokum...housewives terrors. It's almost alarmist, and there's no possible way it can be true."

"You didn't feel something strange...something otherworldly about the objects we've been competing for all this time?"

"That's beside the point. Treasure hunter's euphoria and nothing more. You're reading into the bewilderment of finding something as significant as we have and finding the divine."

"Well," Shakespeare was clearly relishing the moment: "If that is the case, why are you trying so damned hard to stop us?"

"Professionalism. These artifacts should be put to good use. To be learnt from. Marlowe had the right idea, but you seem to think otherwise."

"Don't make me laugh. You're as curious about them as I am. How can we possibly understand these things from behind a glass window? It's like separating yourself from the search of fact by putting a wall between fact and truth. Besides, the mythology fascinates you."

"Fascinates, maybe. Intrigues, yes. Inspires belief? No."

"You should open your mind a little more to the impossible, Pinter. Strange things happen every day. These artifacts included. Isn't it terrific how they haven't seemed to age? Even the Stone of Fal has a gleam to it, as if the stone was polished yesterday."

Pinter let a moment pass before he allowed a response to rush out. The last thing he'd expected from Shakespeare had been a philosophical conversation.

"You may be right," he relented. "But you're still crazy."

"Crazy is as crazy does," Bill sighed. "But deep down, you believe. I can tell. You and I are eerily alike, you know. Cut from the same cloth. Albeit different sides."

"Don't flatter yourself."

"I'm not," Shakespeare laughed. "It's true. Perhaps that's why you make such a good adversary. You're exactly like me, but with a heightened sense of moral judgment. Unfortunately, that's where you fall down and I rise up. You're too afraid to take chances that will cast you into a shadow. I've taken plenty and I'm proud of the fact."

Pinter shrugged, and sipped some more tea as he made himself more comfortable in the chair. Under normal circumstances, the canvas deck-chair would have been his last choice of seat, but after a few days locked in the boot of a car, it was the most comfortable place he could imagine being.

Shakespeare scared him. But only because he was absolutely right – deep down, Pinter knew that there could be no truthful basis for the myth, that it was a ghost story and nothing more, but he'd felt something with the treasures. Something he couldn't begin to explain, even to himself. Some sort of unfathomable greater power. What terrified him most was the accuracy of his opponent's remarks.

He couldn't help but imagine that in a different world, he and Bill Shakespeare could be quite good friends.

"I'm sorry about Dr Randle," Shakespeare said after a time, his voice filled with uncharacteristic sincerity. "I've heard that he was an excellent teacher. Tirey thought very highly of him, too. I've been made to understand he was like a father to you after your own died. He shouldn't have been killed, not for this."

"You killed him. Stop pretending you have some sort of leverage...and leave my father out of this." Pinter replied bluntly, his tone icy. Though his words were cold, his blood boiled.

"If I'd have had my way, he'd still be alive. He was a good man. Unfortunately, Mr Lestate is a poor judge of character and too far removed for regret. His fingers are itchy on his trigger. I, on the other hand, am terribly sorry for your loss."

"Not as sorry as I am."

"Naturally. I recall that Chinese proverb. Randle didn't choose his quitting time. It chose him. Have you chosen yours?"

"That depends entirely on the stakes."

"Is that so? And what stakes would limit you?"

"You don't want to know. Where the hell are we?" Pinter changed the subject as blatantly as he could.

"That would be telling." Shakespeare was clearly warming to his game. "But we won't be here for long. My employers are assembled so our wait is over. We dismantle now and then make our way to a train with supplies waiting to take us swiftly to the coast. Then on and to the island. Our final destination in this little adventure."

"What island?"

"All in good time, Rupert. If you make it that far. Perhaps I've said too much already." He smiled. "Mr Lestate, take Mr Pinter to his girlfriend. I'm sure she's dying to see him."

"I'll be seeing you again soon, I imagine, Bill," Pinter grinned sarcastically as Roach's strong hands dragged him away.

"I wouldn't doubt it for a moment, my dear fellow." Shakespeare smiled to himself as they went out.

It's wonderful to have a nemesis, he thought. *I've waited long enough.*

Picking up a shiny red apple from the platter before him, he took a hearty bite, thinking deeply to himself as he chewed. Pinter had shown himself to be quite the resourceful chap. In any other circumstance, he could use a man like that around. It would, of course, make his job considerably easier.

It was just a shame, he thought, a damn shame that his employers had insisted that the boy be killed before they left the camp.

"Well," he said to himself in the loneliness of the tent. "Things without all remedy should be without regard. What's done is done, I suppose."

He picked up a book, planted himself back in his deck chair, and poured himself another cup of tea as he licked a finger and turned the page.

TWENTY-SEVEN

It was only once Pinter had been tied up with his back to her that Lana finally took mercy enough to glance over her shoulder. She muttered angrily: "Where the hell have you been?"

"Busy."

"Is that right? I can smell tea on you, you know. And pastry. Or is it coffee? Did you enjoy your breakfast with Bill and the lads this morning?"

"As a matter of fact, I did. They really are stand-up chaps," he rolled his eyes. "Where on earth are we?"

"No idea."

"You didn't think to look for road-signs on the way?"

"I didn't get the chance. Why didn't you look, if it's so important to you to know where we are?"

"I've been locked in the boot of one of the cars for the last two days, Lana. The opportunity seemed to elude me. I am sorry for the inconvenience my imprisonment has caused you."

She seemed to soften up: "Oh. I see. Well then, what do we do, Rupert?"

"Rupert? I know I'm in trouble when you use my full name."

"We're both in fairly deep trouble here."

"I doubt it." Pinter shrugged against his bindings, working his wrists in rotation in an attempt to get loose, but feeling only the burn of rope on naked skin. "We'll find a way out, don't worry."

"How? Have you got any great ideas, or just being reassuring?"

"Well...I hadn't thought that far ahead yet, to be honest with you. Give me a moment at least, sweetheart."

"Don't call me sweetheart." She sighed angrily and shifted her weight to get more comfortable, positioning herself so that it was evident she was ignoring him. Pinter didn't notice and instead sat completely still, his eyes closed and the cogs in his mind whirring. The ropes were too tight to slip out of, but he had enough movement in his hand to do something with it, even if it wasn't very much. The only question was what exactly he *could* do.

Think, Pinter. Think.

"Did they treat you alright?" He asked as he struggled against the ropes, trying to force his hand free. Maybe the conversation would help him concentrate on the monotony of escaping being tied up.

She nodded: "For the most part. That Roach Lestate creep has relentlessly wandering hands. I wondered if he'd ever stop accidentally brushing his hand up my skirt."

"Looking at him, it doesn't surprise me a bit."

"And Shakespeare makes my skin crawl."

"Again," he grunted, fighting the burn of the ropes. "...not a surprise. I'm glad you're ok, Lana. Sorry about all this."

"It was my choice to come."

"And I shouldn't have let you. Look where we ended up."

"So you regret bringing me?" He couldn't see it, but her bottomless grey eyes flecked with anger and she bit her bottom lip to prevent herself from saying something stronger.

"Not at all," he smiled, taking her words in good spirits. "You're a great companion to have along. I wouldn't have come with anyone else. I just regret the danger I've put you in since you found me in the library, that's all."

Again, she softened: "What are you doing back there? You're going to throw my hair out of shape if you carry on. And the least you can do if you want to touch my backside is to ask nicely. I'd probably say no, but you could ask anyway just to be polite."

"I think I get can out of these ropes," he answered, ignoring the second half of her complaint as he was so unsure of how to answer it. "They seem loose enough."

Wait a minute...

Something suddenly hit him, a thought crashing through his consciousness like a sledgehammer through glass: "Can you reach your lighter?"

"I think so," her eyes lit up. "Good idea, Roop!"

The way that their hands had been tied behind their backs made the manœuvers extremely difficult, but after some effort Lana managed to slip her Ronson cigarette lighter out of her jacket pocket and place it into Pinter's waiting hand. He flicked it on, and held the flame against the bonds. Smoke rose as the rope burned away, and though he cursed loudly when the naked flame glanced his thumb, he was free considerably faster than he'd expected. He untied his legs and pushed himself to his feet, massaging his wrists: "I never thought I'd be grateful that your father had the sense to buy you a lighter. That wouldn't have worked with matches."

"Very funny," she muttered. "I'll bet you're pleased I have a 'dirty habit' now, aren't you? Take your time, by the way."

He nodded and knelt down before her, untying her feet fist and pulling her up, before turning her back to him so that he could un-tie the bonds on her hands. She spun round to face him and planted quick kiss on his lips. "Thank you."

They took in their surroundings properly for the first time. They were in a tent at the back of the camp. A desk stood at one corner, devoid of any use, and an unused lantern hung from the roof. A single sentry sat outside but never so much as moved his head in their general direction, so Pinter guessed it wouldn't be too much trouble slipping out unnoticed. If they could avoid the party sent to search for them for long enough then perhaps they could get away clean. Shakespeare's men would more than likely give up looking after a short-lived pursuit, especially if they were due to be moving out.

Which, he supposed, would mean their occupancy of the tent had a time limit.

Wonderful, he thought. *Just five minutes to think would be nice!*

His hand went instinctively to his revolver, not registering that his belongings had been taken at Hellfire Castle.

No bag, no gun – all he had left were the contents of his pockets and his flat cap, so with a sense of hope, he searched his trousers to see what he had hidden away.

To his dismay, all he had was a scrap of parchment wrapped carefully in cloth.

His mind rushed back to the Passage of the Dancers, to the Dagda Expedition. The chill of the air in Wales sent a shiver down his spine.

The parchment in the Cauldron. At the time, he hadn't thought anything of it, and merely kept it on him for safekeeping. He must've forgotten all about it, but now it suddenly made perfect sense. He held it up so that Lana could see it, calling to her in hushed tones: "Look!"

"What? What is it?"

"I picked this up when I was in Wales."

"You didn't hand it in after the expedition? *Rupert!*"

"I had a busy couple of days. Besides, I thought it was just an ancient doodle. It's a map, just like the one in the dungeon!"

"Doesn't look much like a map to me."

"Look closer. Shakespeare said they were heading to an island. I think this map shows us where it is."

"How do they know where it is?"

"The runes on the Sword of Nuadu, the lines of the Stone of Fal, and there was a parchment beneath the Spear that I wrapped it in. I hadn't even noticed it. They've known where we were going all along." He kicked himself: "How could I be so blind?"

"Stop feeling sorry for yourself, Roop. Besides, there are no volcanic islands off the British Isles. Not with prominent volcanoes, anyway. So where is it?"

"Think about it. The Tuatha De Danann supposedly congregated in Ireland. So the island on the map must be off the coast of Ireland. And if we look closely, it's right between Ireland and Cornwall, in the middle of the Celtic Sea!"

"There is no island between Ireland and Cornwall."

"Maybe there wasn't, but there is now."

"We would have heard about it by now," she rolled her eyes. "And besides, why is it on an island? Why not just go the mainland. That seems more sensible to me, anyway."

"Who knows?" He shrugged. "I'll expect that one of the areas on the island is sacred. Either way, if we're going to see this through to the end, then we need to get to that island."

"You know," Lana started, wrapping her arms around him: "I think this sort of lifestyle suits you. And you're only just warming to it, aren't you?"

"It seems so," he winked, taking her hand to pull her to the other side of the tent. As he did so, he whispered into her ear: "Come on, we need to go."

They ducked under the canopy of the tent and started for the thick brush that lined the camp. Though the temptation to look back was present in both of their minds, they knew all too well that they simply didn't have time. Pinter pushed Lana on, and they took off down a path that led into a wooded area, willing their footsteps to be inaudible and their breathing quieter. Any moment, the sentry could look round, just out of curiosity at the sudden silence in the tent, and discover his charge had vanished without a trace.

On his way through the camp, heading to the tent on the fringes where he'd left the captives under armed guard, Roach Lestate couldn't help but smile to himself. While in the back of his mind it seemed feeble to harbour such a grudge against someone almost a decade younger than himself, Roach had never been the forgiving kind. Shakespeare had made it perfectly clear that it should be done quickly, but Lestate had absolutely no intention of letting Pinter have it done with that easily.

He wanted to see the terror in the boy's eyes, hear the crunch of broken bones as he returned the favour for his crooked nose. And now would be his chance.

He fingered the knife on his belt tentatively, wondering

joyously to himself where would be the best place to cut, or at least the best place to start cutting. Tongues were fun, but then the screaming would be more subdued. Maybe a finger or an eye. The whole idea of torture fascinated him, filling his twisted mind with strange curiosities that he was more than eager to quench a thirst for.

His smile widened. Perhaps this was the talent he'd been hoping to find his entire life. He was never academic, and boxing was more of a pass-time than a sport to him, but the thought of being an expert at torture made him smile like a Cheshire cat.

Then, as he swept aside the tent flap, ready to begin, the smile on his face turned to a snarl. They were gone.

They were bloody gone.

His blood boiled, and he launched himself at the sentry stood outside by the neck, throttling the man to within an inch of his life as he bellowed at the top of his lungs: "Where are they?!"

The sentry managed to choke a reply, his voice intense with fright: "Inside, sir?"

Roach lifted the man like a doll, clean off the ground, and threw him into the tent, sending the guard sliding across the dirt floor and into a tangle of severed ropes. "Doesn't look like it, does it?"

TWENTY-EIGHT

They hadn't made it very far when the first shouts of alarm echoed over the roofs of the tents. Whoever had discovered they were gone must have been only moments behind them, thought Pinter, which didn't bode well for their escape plan. It didn't bode well for them at all, in fact. Knowing their luck of late they'd have a matter of seconds before a bullet skimmed above their heads and they were led reluctantly back to the camp.

He looked behind them, in time to spot the first machine-gun toting mercenary stumble into sight. He grabbed Lana and pulled her with him into a thick bush, clamping his hand over her mouth in a vain attempt to keep her silent. They ducked low, crouching to be hidden fully by the fauna, just as the mercenary was joined by others. Though they paused for a moment, muttering between themselves about which path it would be best to proceed along, they followed him into the forest beyond, passing perilously close to the hiding place. They were oblivious to the prey hiding beneath their very noses.

Pinter could smell the vodka on their breaths, and hoped that it was a good sign. If they were drinking this early in the morning, it meant one of two things – either they were Russian, which meant they'd be capable of shooting them dead regardless, or they were fools who wouldn't be able to hold a rifle straight, let alone use it properly. He prayed for the latter, but the wafting sounds of harsh Russian vowels travelling on the wind ruined any measure of hope.

Once he was certain they were gone, Pinter moved his hand away from Lana's mouth and took her by the wrist. They stepped quietly out of their hiding place and took a look down the path. They could see the Russians wandering away.

Pinter breathed a momentary sigh of relief and adjusted his hat.

"Do you think we're safe?" Lana whispered, doing her level best to keep her voice as inaudible as possible.

"Not particularly." The reply came from behind them, a voice that leveled equal degrees of menace, frustration and amusement towards them. Shakespeare lifted his Luger into plain sight, making it clear who exactly was in control of the situation. "Nice try, though. Top marks for effort."

They were led back into the camp by five or six of the hired guns, into the flurry of activity as tents were cast down and boxes packed away into waiting Bedford trucks. The small army Shakespeare had assembled was on the move.

The convoy came to a halt in the middle of the camp, a clearing that had obviously been used as a sort of officer's mess. Marks crisscrossed the floor where decking had been lain down and huddled together were a collection of gas canisters, heavy enough to be left until last as far as the mercenaries loading up their trucks were concerned.

Roach, who had been pushing Pinter with varying force on their way back into camp, shoved the younger man to the ground, sending Pinter sprawling into one of the canisters. The impact knocked the heavy petrol can over, and brown fuel oozed onto the ground. Miraculously untouched by the petroleum, Pinter pitched himself up and looked down the barrel of Shakespeare's drawn gun.

"So you're going to kill me yourself now? Good for you. I was worried you'd let your lackey do all the dirty work. At least now I know that you're not afraid to get your hands dirty, Bill."

"I'm afraid so, old boy," Shakespeare shrugged. "Orders are orders, after all."

"You'll be doing yourself a favour," Pinter spat.

"I'm well aware."

"Even if this does all turn out to be true...even if the Tuatha De Danann return and they open up the gates to the Otherworld...even if Hell descends...you're still being played for a fool." Pinter felt the cold steel of the Luger glance his chin and the searing, hot pain course through his skull as the impact stopped him from saying any more and knocked him sideways. He collided with the dusty floor with a thud and coughed mud. Looking back up at Shakespeare with blood streaming from a cut in his cheek, he spat: "I'm right, then?"

"Kill him. I can't be bothered to do it myself." The words were reassured and calculated, but Pinter knew that Shakespeare simply couldn't bear to do the deed. He'd hit the nail on the head, and Bill's ego was nicely bruised. "Take him behind the tents and kill him there. Out of my sight."

Pinter smiled cockily, fear driving his arrogance. Blood trickled down his chin from the gap in his gum where his tooth had finally come loose and disappeared onto the dusty floor.

Never mind, he thought. *I won't need it now anyway.*

"Cheerio then, Bill. Lana," she looked at him, her eyes glistening with tears and her pupils wide in terror. He winked: "I'll be right back."

A pair of mercenaries grabbed him by the arms and lifted him to his feet, dragging him away. He didn't fight them, choosing instead to give Shakespeare an amused look as he was carried away. Roach quietly burned, fury eating his gut: "He was mine."

"Calm down, Roach. He was nothing."

"What about the girl?" Lestate nodded to Lana, who was being held back by one of the hired guns and who struggled helplessly to get free and go to Pinter's side.

"She'll have to come with us. Load the cars."

"Why don't we just kill her and have done with it?" A smile crept across Roach's crimson face. Perhaps he'd have his taste of murder after all. "It will save us a great deal of effort. This one bites."

"We don't need to spill anymore blood."

Roach rolled his eyes: "Is that so?" He pulled Shakespeare to one side and spoke in hushed tones: "You should stop thinking about having the girl for yourself, Bill. She isn't the prize, and we have a job to do. She'll just get in the way."

As they turned away from her, Lana realised exactly what Pinter had done in his display of arrogant heroics. Her lighter lay on the floor, and acting as though she were still struggling, she hooked it closer with her toe and hid it beneath her foot.

Shakespeare straightened up and attempted to assert his importance by turning to Roach and replying loudly enough for Lana to hear: "You know something, Mr

Lestate? You're absolutely right."

He drew his Luger and spun round, aiming at Lana's head.

She shook the thugs off as they stepped away.

"At least let me have a cigarette before you kill me, Bill. It's a matter of chivalry. I thought that you of all people would have some respect for that."

She'd hit the nail on the head. Killing women wasn't his forte, he had to admit to himself, but if it had to be done then it would be done properly and with the correct etiquette.

He nodded: "Very well."

As she pulled a cigarette out of the packet she fumbled, dropping it and falling to her knees to retrieve it from the ground. As she did so, she picked up the Ronson lighter and flicked it on. By the time she was upright, she had placed the cigarette gracefully between her lips. Looking directly into Shakespeare's eyes, she took a long draw on the stick.

The two mercenaries pushed Pinter against a tree behind the tents. Turning him around to face them, they withdrew to a few paces away and leveled their rifles.

They aimed, ready to fire.

The harsh crack of the guns being cocked forced Pinter to throw his hands into the air in a classic surrender pose, managing to stammer in broken Russian: "You don't have to do this!"

The firing squad exchanged a bemused glance.

Think, Pinter told himself. *The mental phrasebook, damnit.*

The heavier set of the two mercenaries spoke up, his English slow and carefully considered, even though he put emphasis on the wrong words: "How do you know Russian?"

"I had a Russian aunt," Pinter lied, still in Russian but struggling even more now. "She was an excellent drinker."

"You are good. It is a shame," the second man said, in Russian now. Pinter could only imagine that he had no grasp of English at all. "Orders are orders."

Pinter's mind raced. This couldn't be it. They'd come so far, and yet he had so much left that he wanted to do.

Surely this wasn't the end?

Oh, great.

"Any last words?"

Though his mind fought to find something poignant, something memorable or significant, Pinter could only think of one thing to say.

"Oh, shit."

"You know, my father is an important man," Lana bragged between bursts of smoke. "He'll hunt you down even if it takes him forever. Besides, can you live with yourself for what you're about to do? I mean…" she winked, though discomfort rocketed through her. "Look at me!"

Shakespeare shrugged. "There are plenty more women. As for your father…I can't imagine him being difficult to rid myself of. He was useless on board the zeppelin. Besides, for all you know the world could end tomorrow, anyway. I'm offering a hero's way out."

Lana shrugged back at him. She only had a drag left.

It was now or never.

With one slick motion, she flicked the cigarette towards the spilt petrol. Hundreds of cigarettes worth of practice informed her aim, and the glimmering red arched slowly downwards.

It was only after the point of no return had been passed that Shakespeare realised with horror the open flame landing on the fuel.

The combustion was shocking, blowing the pile of canisters to pieces and sending debris flying as the nearby tents burst into flames. As the camp went up, Lana hit the deck, covering her face, avoiding the sight of a mercenary caught in the blast being catapulted skywards, his arms writhing as, while airborne, he tried to extinguish himself.

Shakespeare grabbed Lana by the arm and pulled her away from the firestorm as the entire camp went up, a raging inferno that towered about them and threatened to trap them inside.

TWENTY-NINE

The radius of the blast sent a shockwave tearing through the encampment, knocking the executioners clean off their feet and sending them toppling sideways. It afforded Pinter a glimmering moment in which he was able to lunge perilously forward and land a perfect sucker-punch to the face of the nearest gunman. Fist and jaw connected with a sickening crunch, and the burly Russian fell like a sack of potatoes, the rifle slipping from his hand as he lost consciousness before even reaching the floor.

As he fell, Pinter tore the rifle from his fingers and swung it in a well-practiced tennis player's arch into the approaching face of the second goon, landing with an ear-splitting thud. He could hardly believe his luck, and for a moment stood between the two unconscious bodies with his jaw hanging open in surprise, before shaking his head quickly and focusing on the task in hand.

The rifle he now held was loaded and the safety was off, but nevertheless he gave himself a moment to level it and judge the weight of the weapon in his shaking hands. Ahead of him lay the remains of the camp, alive with screaming and shouting and the crackle of rapidly spreading flames, which bounced majestically from tent to tent. He took a deep breath, then, with a burst of cautious confidence, hopped over the collapsed tent that sat between him and the maelstrom and headed into the blazing inferno.

It was chaos, as if the whole world was on fire around them. Tents fell apart everywhere he looked, smoldering and popping as flames licked charred canvas. Men ran to and fro, carrying boxes and undamaged supplies to the trucks waiting nearby. The engines were running and waiting to tear off down the dirt track away from the camp.

If the flames got too close, it could mean the vehicles would go up too, and that was the last thing anyone wanted to happen.

He scanned the area for Lana, finally spotting her as she was dragged to a flat-bed truck on the other side of the camp. Everything was moving too quickly for him to register, and before he'd even started moving towards Shakespeare and his entourage, the last few hired guns hopped into vehicles and took off.

Pinter dropped the rifle and ran as fast as he could towards Lana and her snarling escorts.

"Lana!" Her head spun in his direction and he couldn't have been more than a few metres away when she yelled back: two words that filled him with instant dread.

"Look out!"

The impact was like being hit by a speeding freight train, sending the wind rushing out of him as he hit the ground. He felt chubby fingers claw at his hair and drag him back upright.

With horror Pinter found himself looking into the

bloodshot, venomous eyes of Roach Lestate, who grinned wildly as he drew his fist back. The punch sent Pinter's neck snapping backwards. As his eyes watered with pain his body fell with the impact, launching him backwards and sending him sprawling to the floor.

Rolling now, so that Roach couldn't grab him, Pinter pushed himself back to his feet, spitting blood as he stumbled into a boxer's pose, fists raised and clenched and his feet pawing the ground.

Stars danced before his eyes. The best that would come of this would be that Roach would land him back in the dentist's chair, even if he ended up as the victor.

He tried not to consider the worst possible outcome. Losing the fight wasn't really an option, and Roach didn't seem like the kind of fellow that would accept a white-flag in surrender. He meant to do some very serious damage.

He had murder on his mind.

His attacker smiled sardonically and cockily Pinter grinned back, though inside fear gripped him like a closed vice. If their last encounter was anything to go by, Roach would treat him like a ragdoll, and this time there was no quick escape route by jumping into a river. It didn't quite work that way with fire. If he could get out of this one without a broken nose, he figured, he'd be one up on the thug.

Roach leapt forward, but, quick on his toes, Pinter danced around the line of attack and delivered a blow that glanced Roach's chin, sending the man sideways. He stumbled, and Pinter muttered angrily to himself: "You'll find I'm full of surprises."

Roach regained his standing and spat out a tooth as blood-stained gums transformed from a smile to a snarl. His eyes burned with malice. Again he flung himself at Pinter, tackling him to the ground and tearing the flat cap from his head. He threw the hat aside, out of sight.

The two men grappled in the dirt, wild punches bouncing without technique or symmetry, both fighting for all they were worth. Pinter felt enormous fingers tighten around his neck. His flesh was red with pressure.

His air was gone. His face was turning blue.

That can't be good.

Panic started to grip him as he fought against the clamp, the weight of the man pinning him helplessly to the ground. His hand snapped out of the crush of bodies, leaving him open to suffocation, and frantically he scavenged, looking for something he could use.

Anything!

His lungs burned and he felt the world going dark.

A strange numbing sensation filled him. His hand moved sluggishly, but his fingers fumbled over a rock and he clasped it weakly, mustering all the strength he had left.

With Herculean effort he heaved it into Roach's temple.

Groaning, the dazed thug toppled sideways and rolled away. Spluttering and gasping for breath as if he hadn't filled his lungs in years, Pinter forced himself upright, his world spinning, just in time to see Roach shake off the stun of the blow and leap to his own feet.

In the space between punches, Pinter found his opportunity, stepping closer before the stars had stopped dancing before Roach's eyes.

A weak left hook led into a strong right, and though his knuckles were red-raw and ached like hell, Pinter clasped his hands together and flung his balled fists in a stronger left swing directly into Roach's jaw, sending the thug stumbling clumsily backwards.

They circled each other, Roach cutting off the only means of escape for his young opponent, cornering him inside the flaming ruins of the camp.

Feigning left, Roach came in from the right – a meaty punch that met Pinter's skull like an automobile. Pain exploded in Pinter's head and he now stumbled back, feeling the heat of the flames lick his back. Despite the fire, shivers ran down up his spine as he realized that one step back would land him in the inferno. He swallowed deeply.

One wrong move and I'm a dead man, he thought angrily. *So make the right move!*

Roach was elated now, it seemed, kicking his heels in the dirt like a bull ready to charge. Veins in his crimson brow throbbed and blood streamed down his chin.

It struck Pinter that the man now looked like a slobbering bulldog – truly an animal.

Oh Christ, he thought. *Here we go.*

Roach tore at him like lightning, and all Pinter could do was dodge. At the last possible moment, Pinter dove forwards, shielding his skull from the impact, and colliding with Roach's legs.

It was a sensible course of action.

In his arrogance, Roach hadn't given himself room for error and tripped over Pinter, falling headfirst into the flames, his arms flailing in a vain attempt to stop the inevitable plunge into the bonfire. All Rupert could do was watch in horror as the man became tangled in the ropes and canvas of the flaming tent, disappearing into a fiery coffin as a section of the tent collapsed on top of him.

Screams of pain exploded as Roach caught alight, and there was nothing Pinter could do but watch as the man burned to death. Even the pain that ached across his body was nothing but a distant memory as the fire grew hotter and the flames leapt higher, the stench of roasted flesh tickling his nose.

He couldn't think of anything to say, so instead sighed in relief as the confrontation came to a disturbing end.

All at once, there was no sound at all, just the hiss of Roach's hair and clothes burning up. A nasty way to go.

He rubbed his nose. Not broken.

Well, he thought. *That's something.*

Pinter took a look around him as he stepped away, spotting his flat cap crumpled in the dust. He scooped it up and brushed dirt from it, turning it in his hands thoughtfully. Looking up, he followed the direction of the road as it twisted out of sight.

The train station, he reflected. *They were heading to the train station.*

His mind fixed on Lana, and how he was going to go about rescuing her. Nothing else mattered now. Shakespeare could raise the Tuatha De Danann if he wanted, Pinter didn't give a damn, but he sure as hell wasn't going to drag Lana into some sort of occult ceremony. The thought of Lana acting as some pagan sacrifice made him sick to the stomach.

He shook the sinister idea from his mind and bolted to the road.

They were long gone, and it would be impossible to catch them on foot now. He sighed and kicked his heels in the dirt in frustration. As he did, his heel caught something and he looked down in surprise. Below him was his satchel. Smiling, he swung the shoulder bag over his neck and onto his back.

Now what?

A whinny drew his attention. Evidently not planning for a speedy evacuation, the fools had left hitched horses tethered to a post, clear of the blaze but abandoned nonetheless.

Pinter crushed his hat onto his head, a cocky grin creasing his jaw. "Well..." he muttered to himself. "Here we go..."

THIRTY

Shakespeare cut purposefully through the bedlam as his men frantically loaded the last of the supply boxes onto the waiting freight carriages. The train at the head of the convoy, a black and green steam locomotive, hissed and smoked relentlessly - the mechanical dragon alive and furious. Roughly, he pushed Lana up some steps and into the dining car, locking the door behind her. He turned away and straightened his lapels, ignoring the crack of fists against the wood and glass as she fought in vain to escape.

"Calm down," he muttered glumly as one of his subordinates jogged through a cloud of steam, pacing down the platform towards him.

"No sign of Mr Lestate, sir."

"Then we'll have to go without him." Shakespeare was disappointed. He'd expected better than Roach to have been bested by a child. But these things happened, he supposed. It was his own fault really – he should have taken care of Pinter himself.

He answered without looking at the mercenary – one of the few who actually spoke fluent English – focusing instead on the activity along the platform: "Where is Chaucer?"

"In your carriage, sir. As you instructed."

"Good. Take the girl in there and keep an eye on them both. We're far too close now to have one of them throw a spanner in the works."

A whistle blew, the piercing shriek echoing through the smoke-thick air. Shakespeare removed his hunting helmet, handed it to the mercenary, and once again smoothed his lapels. He smiled with a degree of discomfort that he managed to hide from the hired gun who bounced nervously on his toes. "I'll be along. Get the men on board. I'll be on board before the train leaves the station. I'm simply..." he paused, thinking carefully about how best to phrase it: "...concerned."

"Yes, sir!"

The pangs of anxiety sent the hairs on Shakespeare's back rocketing skywards as the last few men swung themselves up the ladders and into the train cars. Pinter was a damn sight more resourceful than he'd given him credit for. And it would seem that the boy was good in a fight too. Roach was a brick of a man, a being of pure muscle with more brawn than brain. Pinter must have something going for him to have come out on top.

Unless they'd killed each other. Or Roach was simply left behind.

He didn't want to take a chance though. Rupert Pinter had surprised him before, and now he was on his toes. The last thing he wanted to do was underestimate the boy again. Another mistake like that could derail the whole operation.

There was a screech as the locomotive began to roll painfully forwards, so, shrugging off the concerns of his opponent, Shakespeare mounted the carriage. Despite himself, a nagging, horrible feeling possessed him to hang onto the iron rungs of the ladder, leaning out so that he could see the station as they moved out. He supposed that it was just in case his young friend decided to make a last minute dash to prevent himself from missing the train. As the steam dissipated and it became clear that Pinter was nowhere near the convoy, Shakespeare finally allowed a luxurious moment of relief. He pulled himself up and into the carriage and took up his seat opposite Lana as the train thundered into the countryside.

On a ridge above the train station, hidden by thick bushes and out of sight, Pinter looked down upon the small army as it departed. He'd arrived in the nick of time, dismounting as the last box was thrown aboard and the carriage doors slammed shut. Fortunately, his tardiness had given him enough time to watch Shakespeare for a moment, time enough to study the look of growing fear. The relief that followed had a sense of irony to it, and Pinter couldn't help but smile. If only he knew.

But what if he does? Pinter felt his brow furrow subconsciously. *Not that it matters now, anyway.*

The train was out of the station and disappearing into the hills as he swung his leg over the saddle and reigned in, stroking the horse's mane to calm it as the animal shuddered at the sound of the piercing whistle cutting over the brim of the hills ahead. The trek had been swift and comfortable. The horse was more than capable as they followed the trail of debris that had been strewn into the road, presumably by the trucks hitting potholes sending poorly secured supplies leaping skywards. He imagined he was a mere few minutes behind them when he'd arrived at his vantage point.

The horse whinnied in protest as Pinter adjusted his hat, kicked his heels and whipped the reins. They took off, tearing through the terrain as they descended along the path towards the railway line.

Aboard his carriage, Shakespeare took a sip from a cup of tea and studied Christoph Chaucer's nervous twitch. It was a strange one, isolated to just below the right temple, and it throbbed constantly as Chaucer did his best to avoid eye-contact, keeping his pupils trained on the countryside as the train bounced along the tracks. Shakespeare wouldn't even have noticed it if it hadn't been for the way the man was constantly wringing his hands and fiddling with his cigarette case, turning it over and over between his thin fingers.

"Would you stab your own mother in the back for a quick handful of cash?"

Chaucer swallowed audibly and began to fidget with more ferocity as Shakespeare watched him: "What are you trying to suggest, *mon ami?*"

"That you're a slimy, nasty piece of work, if I'm being perfectly honest. I can imagine you'd find it simpler to sell out a sibling than your parents, though. If you were offered a bar of gold to cut out your brother's tongue, how long would it take for you to draw your blade?"

"I resent that."

"I'm sure you do, *mon ami,*" Shakespeare said with gleeful venom, stressing the French. "I've no doubt of that at all."

"Without me, my dear Mr Shakespeare, you would not have retrieved the Spear of Lug."

Shakespeare snorted: "You had nothing to do with it. If I recall correctly, it was Rupert Pinter that led us to the last of the four treasures. You may well have suggested a starting point, but it was Pinter that was resourceful enough to retrieve the treasure from the Guardians of the Tuatha De Danann."

"The Guardians are a mere myth."

"One that you and I have both seen with our own eyes. If evidence of *that* myth is enough to prove the Four Treasures of the Tuatha De Danann are what you've spent so many years trying to convince your fellow academics that they are, then perhaps you've earned enough of a payment already," Shakespeare baited. "Perhaps I need not pay you for what limited assistance you've provided after all."

"Nevertheless," Chaucer stammered: "You will need me to proceed. There is more to the Gates of the Otherworld than simply a lock and key."

"That's common sense, Mr Chaucer. Sadly, my employers are men much more learned in the ancient druid ways than you. In fact, I'm amazed they allowed you to remain alive for such an extended period of time. As far as they're be concerned, you wouldn't even know how to place the key in the lock, much less *turn* the key."

Chaucer went white as Shakespeare sighed and calmly sipped his tea. He was taking great pleasure in making the Frenchman squirm.

"Perhaps they pity you. Perhaps they wanted to keep you alive long enough to see what a fool you have been. You've spent your whole life searching for the treasures of the Tuatha De Danann and found nothing, whereas I have managed to recover all the pieces in a matter of months. It's shameful really."

The horse reared as it attacked the gravel beside the track, and Pinter felt a pang of terror as the animal threatened to buck. He shrugged it off as the horse settled, then set its nose low and galloped after the train.

They were gaining ground a lot more quickly than he'd imagined they would, but he knew that the stamina of the horse couldn't hold out for much longer. He'd have a few minutes at best to get alongside the train and jump aboard, and if he didn't manage to do it before they hit an incline, the horse would either collapse, or throw him off in mutiny.

The train wasn't going particularly fast yet, but a comparatively speedy rate even for the powerful animal he sat atop, which strained to keep going. As an inexperienced rider, Pinter gripped the front of the saddle for dear life and kept his head low against the wind, which buffered him relentlessly. He kept his breathing short as they reached the clouds of smoke exploding from the stack of the locomotive, desperate not to choke. If he lost concentration now, then this would all have been for nothing.

He set his jaw, doing his level best to focus.

Before he knew it, he was alongside the rear carriage, a poorly maintained brake car which clattered as though it was about to fall to pieces bouncing against the weathered railway. Though his body shook with fear, he reached out with his free hand, keeping the other clamped to the saddle like a vice.

He'd have to attempt to grab the iron railing on the back of the car. The horse fought against how close they were to the moving train, and though his fingertips brushed metal, he couldn't reach close enough for a decent grasp. Pinter muttered calming phrases to his steed before pulling on the reins, bringing them closer and reaching again.

This time the horse really fought, and Pinter suddenly realised why as he looked up.

Ahead of them the ground fell away as the train hit a bridge.

"Great..." he said aloud to himself, feeling his skin going white.

All he could do was hoist himself further up in the saddle, so he did, figuring that maybe it would give him a fractionally shorter distance to reach for the rung of the brake car.

Inches away now. No luck.

The access ladder on the side of the train was marginally closer, so he went for that.

His fingers brushed metal again. The drop drew closer.

One more try.

His palm was wet with fear, and he knew this was it.

One last chance.

Come on, he willed himself. *This is child's play.*

He made a grab as the ground fell away, launching himself from the saddle as the horse bucked.

The nothingness for a considerable distance below him became all too evident. His legs dangled above the ravine helplessly, and he felt his heart race as the full weight of his body threatened to drag him into it.

THIRTY-ONE

Pinter swung his body onto the access ladder, his hand firmly clamped onto the iron rung. The train left safety and thundered onto the thin wooden bridge that crossed the sharp drop over the ravine. Far below, a river snaked its way to the sea.

Something to cushion my fall, I suppose, Pinter thought.

They were heading into the mountains now. Despite the smoke belching from the locomotive up ahead the air seemed clean and refreshing.

He scaled the ladder and climbed onto the roof of the brake car. Though the speed of the train was limited, for a perilous moment he almost lost his footing. The idea of falling towards the severe drop below caused him to drop to his knees, which in turn counter-acted the toppling motion, sending him sprawling onto his face. Grunting in pain, he pushed himself back to his knees and began crawling along the roof, his eyes set on the locomotive which trundled along about three carriages ahead of him.

He'd already clocked the carriage that Lana was being held in, and it sat directly behind the steam engine, so all he had to do was edge his way across the three rail-cars, avoid being seen, then swing inside and ask politely for Lana back. He patted his gun, just to check it was still there.

It was all too simple, really. He grinned to himself: "Here goes nothing."

The train bounced on the worn rails as it left the bridge and hit the mountain line, safety appearing on either side. They were in a valley now, trough-like as the line cut deep into the hills and walls seemed to grow on either side. Ahead of him the line twisted round a corner and out of sight, an image framed by the views of the mountains. It would have been quite beautiful if he wasn't in quite so much danger.

He tried to ignore it and carried on crawling forwards. Silence was key now, as the car ahead was a passenger bearing carriage in a former life with windows lining either side. He had no doubt that there would be a garrison full of mercenaries occupying the car, so biting his tongue he reached for the edge of the carriage. This time the transfer was considerably easier, and he hoisted himself onto the roof, wordlessly congratulating himself. The wind wasn't quite so bad now with the shelter either side. He started to move forwards, crouching low but on his feet.

Another jolt as the train hit a bad section of track slammed his teeth together and the shock knocked him back to his chest, sending him sprawling again. Ahead, he caught sight of a low hanging tunnel, wide at either side but barely low enough for the carriage to get through, let alone a stowaway passenger occupying a seat on the roof.

It was gaining ground far too quickly for comfort. Pinter felt a bead of sweat trace his brow.

Too close.

Far too close. The locomotive disappeared inside. Then the first carriage.

The second was gone almost instantly.

It was as if time suddenly sped up.

The nose of his carriage edged inside, and as the whistle howled, ringing through the tunnel like a hell-bound shriek, Pinter swung himself to the side and hung from the edge of the carriage, inches away from decapitation. He breathed a heavy sigh of relief before the smoke trapped in the tunnel engulfed him and gritted his teeth through muscle burn as he looked through the window at the collection of mercenaries inside.

Fear took hold of him as he realised they could see him.

None had, yet, as they seemed too engrossed in conversation to notice, but surely one would look in his direction in a moment, he guessed. His heart raced.

Sunlight hit his back as they emerged again from the tunnel, and at the very moment that Pinter began to pull himself back onto the roof, he caught the eye of one of the soldiers inside.

There was a strange moment where the mercenary stared in disbelief.

Pinter smiled.

The mercenary smiled back.

He was clearly impressed by the sight of a young man holding onto the side of a train for dear life, patting one of his colleagues on the shoulder and pointing. Laughter followed.

But not for long – his hand went to his holster and his gun flashed into view.

Pinter hauled himself back onto the roof as the window shattered and a bullet skimmed the toe of his boot. His heart pounded against his chest as though his lungs were timpani drums. He fumbled for his revolver as the first mercenary climbed out of the smashed window and onto the roof.

Pinter had barely got his footing back when the first punch traced his jaw, sending his head in the right direction to see his gun toppling helplessly over the side of the train. Bringing his fists up into a boxer's pose, he volleyed left – too slow on the uptake to do any damage, and giving the mercenary an opportunity to land a well aimed blow to his gut.

Pinter reeled and almost toppled over, but the momentum of the wind against his back allowed him to swing back at the mercenary with a powerful sucker-punch right to the jaw, which sent the unprepared man tumbling over the side of the train with a look of surprise spread over his face as his final expression.

Pinter was on the move before he could even consider his luck, leaping athletically over the gap between carriages as bullets ricocheted near his feet. Another mercenary was right behind him, gun drawn, and Pinter went for his Webley.

He could only roll his eyes as he reached into his holster and found nothing there, forgetting for a moment that his gun had disappeared into the mountains forever. All he could do now was run, so he turned on his heel and did so, trying his best not to focus on the bullets whizzing past him and ricocheting off the roof of the carriage. His only option was to drop down into the gap between the carriages and hope that he could somehow catch the man off guard when he came after him. He lowered himself carefully and quickly down and into cover.

He didn't have time to think, as a door beside him opened and another thug came rushing out, his rifle raised in readiness. Pinter grabbed at the barrel and the two wrestled for the gun, fighting each other in the enclosed space, desperate for a chance to throw the other off.

Trying to catch Pinter off guard, the mercenary relinquished the gun and drew his fist back to throw a punch, but anticipating the move, Pinter swung the butt of the rifle into the man's face, knocking him unconscious instantly. The mercenary fell against the door, jamming it shut with his dead-weight.

Pinter looked down at the gun, taking a moment to register that he now had a weapon. When the realisation finally hit him, he reached quickly for the automatic pistol in the mercenary's holster, placed it into his own, and then grabbed onto the rungs of the ladder and went for the roof again, this time the rifle in his hand in readiness.

The gunman on the roof was waiting, however, and before Pinter could bring himself any higher than the top rung sparks showered him as a bullet bounced off the metal. He swore under his breath then went for the roof again. The gun-man was reloading, and seemed to be struggling with the clip. Pinter snorted – there was a reason he didn't normally bother with automatic weapons. He straightened the rifle and went for the shot, depressing the trigger and bracing for the recoil.

There wasn't one.

A hollow click pierced his eardrums.

The gun was jammed.

He fought with the safety for a moment but knew it was too late. While his attacker was also fighting to get his gun working, another man had crept onto the roof. Pinter turned on his heel, figuring it made more sense to gain ground. There were men pouring out of windows and climbing out of doors everywhere now.

But something was odd – none of them were getting up onto the roof.

He focused on the locomotive. He watched it pass under

a low hanging bridge.

A low hanging bridge that was rushing towards him.

"Oh, bugger!" He heard himself yelling at the top of his voice as he flung himself back into cover, centimetres away this time from the bridge catching him.

The rifle snagged on the ends of the carriage roofs, leaving him dangling above the couples beneath as though he'd fallen from a tightrope.

He pulled himself back up to look further down the train. He'd got lucky with his escape, but his two pursuers weren't quite as fortunate. Stone had met skull with a sickening crunch as they collided with the bridge and disappeared into expiration.

"Woah..." Pinter's mouth hung open in surprise as he climbed back onto the train roof, and he had to shrug off the surprise of how close he'd come. Reassuringly, he had the knowledge of what lay before him. The locomotive was directly ahead now, which could only mean that he had managed to reach the carriage Shakespeare was riding in.

Lana had to be below him.

Less reassuring, however, was the sight of the initially reluctant mercenaries now populating the rooftops, drawing their guns and giving chase. He sturdied himself as he drew his newly acquired pistol, a 1902 .38 Colt.

Powerful, but old. The fellow he'd borrowed it from clearly had a taste for old weapons. He could only hope it did the job well and had been kept in decent working order.

He scoped out the positioning of the windows below and found a point of entry as a bullet bounced from the roof near his feet. Taking a deep breath, Pinter found a firm grip on the edge of the carriage. With the gun in his free hand, he swung himself into the breach.

Shakespeare spilled his tea in surprise as glass shattered

and Pinter burst through, gun drawn and ready, crashing down onto the carpeted floor of the carriage. He stumbled clumsily to his feet, aiming directly at Shakespeare's skull as a glass slipped off the table and smashed.

"Sorry I'm late, Bill. I missed the train."

Shakespeare laughed, clearly appreciative of the pun. "Very good. You did away with Roach, then?"

"He had it coming."

"Probably," Shakespeare shrugged. "You've come for your girlfriend, I expect?"

Pinter shot a look over to Lana, who was rising from her chair in the corner. The fool hadn't thought to tie her up or provide any means of hindering their escape.

"Looks like it, doesn't it?" Pinter said, almost cockily, but with a collected, reasonable tone that even Shakespeare would have been proud of. Bill smiled.

"Then what?" There was a vicious pause, which Shakespeare seemed to enjoy a great deal.

His smile was wiped when Pinter deadpanned: "I didn't plan that far ahead."

"That much is evident."

He took Lana's hand and shot Chaucer a disgusted look. The Frenchman cowered.

"Now what will you do?" Shakespeare got to his feet. "You're going to sit here and wait until we reach the station? There's improvisation my boy...and then there's stupidity. This, I'm afraid, is a prime example of the latter."

There was a bang on the door as some of the mercenaries tried to open the locked carriage. Pinter's head snapped sideways to investigate the sound.

They were trapped. Again.

Bugger.

"Good try, old man," Shakespeare sneered. "It's a good thing I locked that door before we left, though, or else this rescue mission would have ended a few minutes ago."

As he took a moment to look out of the window, Pinter's finger tightened on the trigger. Only one thing for it now. They had emerged onto the side of a valley, where the railway line cut into the side of the mountain. On one side of the train was a wall of rock. On the other, a steep, grassy incline...but a grassy incline nonetheless, that rolled down a short distance and into a lake. His mind went over it, weighing up his options. It seemed he had no others. Tearing a map from a table covered with research that he imagined Shakespeare had been collating, he stuffed it into his pocket, before pulling Lana to the access door on the other side of the carriage.

"I'll see you later, Bill," he smirked.

Shakespeare nodded, a sort of grudging respect: "I've no doubt, Pinter."

Slipping open the access door, Pinter and Lana stepped out between the carriage and the locomotive.

As Pinter closed the door and broke the lock with the butt of the pistol, Lana finally reprimanded him: "You took your time!"

"The story of my life," he bellowed against the roar of the steam engine. "Besides, I wish you'd stop saying that!"

He took a look below them. The rails thundered past.

Measuring up the distance between them and the grassy slope, Pinter winced: "This might hurt a bit!"

She looked down: "Oh no. No. No!"

"We don't have a choice!"

"I'd rather go back inside!"

"With him?" Pinter's eyebrow was cocked in surprise.

She thought for a moment. "Good point. Maybe not."

He took her hand and squeezed it. "Ready?"

"Did I ever tell you I'm sorry I ever met you?"

"Sounds about right." He steeled himself. "On three!

One!"
 "Two!" she yelled.
 "Three!"

THIRTY-TWO

Pinter opened one eye slowly.

He was alive, then.

They'd fallen a fair distance in the leap from the train, but as he squinted through tender eyes he could see the last car of the train trundling off into the distance. Bemused mercenaries stood atop pointing and shaking their heads in disbelief at what had just unfolded before them.

Lucky, really, he thought. *They were too busy enjoying the spectacle to shoot us.*

He could just make out the figure of Bill Shakespeare hanging from the side of the train. He'd obviously stuck around to watch the pair as they tumbled down the hill and out of harm's way.

He thought then of Lana, who lay beside him, clasping her hands to her head. She was groaning in pain, but there was no sign of any blood. He hitched himself onto his elbows and leant over her.

"Never again." The words came through gritted teeth.

"That was even less fun than I imagined."

"I don't think I'll be trying that again either," Pinter replied, grimacing. "That was very, very stupid. Very stupid indeed. Are you alright? Have you hurt anything?"

"I'll live. Nothing a hot bath won't fix. How about you?"

Gently, he flexed his fingers. Feeling there. Feeling all over, in fact. So that meant there was nothing broken. Nothing even seriously injured. The grass had broken their fall from the speeding train quite well.

He lifted himself tentatively from his elbows to his feet. Everything seemed to be in order. No broken bones. A bit sore all over, but then that was nothing new. He helped Lana up, and almost instantly she threw her arms around him, hugging him tightly.

"I thought you were dead, you bloody idiot!"

"I've been hearing that a lot lately, it's not something I'd like to hear on a regular basis."

"Shut up." She pulled his mouth to hers and landed a passionate kiss on his lips. Though he was surprised, he wrapped his arms around her in return and held her tight. As she pulled away, a satisfied gasp escaped his lungs:

"Wow."

"Don't worry me like that again."

"If that's the punishment," he grinned, "I may have to do it more often."

She punched him playfully on the arm, and he smiled, turning his attention to the column of smoke that rose up into the sky, far off in the distance now.

"So what's the next big idea, Roop?" he heard Lana say, lost in his own thought process.

"We see this through." He scooped up his hat from the floor and dropped it onto his head. For the first time he realised he still had the map tucked into his pocket and pulled it out, opening it wide enough for her to be able to see: "We're not too far away. Destination is a few miles down the tracks. That would put us here, by the lake, and the small port is where they're going."

"We'll never catch them now. Not on foot. By the time we get there they'll be long gone."

"We can try," he smirked, as out of the corner of his eye he spotted the horse, forgotten in the chaos, trotting eagerly towards them. He couldn't help but chuckle to himself: "Good girl!"

"You were riding that?" Lana didn't seem particularly impressed, but Pinter smiled and shrugged.

"She followed the train. We might just catch them yet." He pulled the horse closer and stroked her nose. "Clever animals, horses. The cleverest. I wish I could keep her."

"Not if I have anything to do with it. I hate horses."

"Didn't your father ever buy you a pony?"

"No. He said it was a terrible idea. I thoroughly agree."

He vaulted onto the horse's back, stroking the mane with a wide grin. Holding out his hand, he motioned to Lana: "Are you coming?"

Lana nodded: "Well I'm not staying here on my own." She took his hand and clambered awkwardly onto the saddle behind Pinter, trying her best to make herself comfortable. "I hate horses."

"*C'est magnifique!*" exclaimed Chaucer as Shakespeare dropped into a chair. "They will never catch us now. There is no chance at all. We're 'home free', as you would say!"

Shakespeare said nothing of the sort, instead fixing himself a large scotch and lime on the rocks. His silence made Chaucer all the more nervous. The Frenchman laughed uncomfortably: "Do you not think, *mon ami*?"

"No." There was a sharp edge to the blunt reply. "They have a map. They know exactly where we're heading."

"*C'est la vie.* They will never catch us!"

"With Rupert Pinter's track record, do you really believe that?" Shakespeare had daggers in his eyes, daggers that seemed to pierce Christoph Chaucer's very being. He felt his blood run cold.

Trying to reassure himself, he attempted feebly to retort: "His luck must run out eventually, *non?*"

"*Non.*" Shakespeare turned to look out of the window, at the approaching coast as the mountains fell away. Beyond, the Isle of the Tuatha De Danann lay waiting.

An odd feeling of pure dread coursed through him, a feeling almost alien, and one that he hadn't felt in a long time in such abundance. He sipped at his drink sullenly. It would all be over in a few hours. Afterwards he'd have nothing more to worry about, but regardless of the confidence he had with how close they were to the finishing line he still had a nasty feeling.

"Get your things," he muttered, downing the tumbler and smacking his lips as the alcohol burned his chest. "We'll be there soon."

They couldn't have been far behind by the time Pinter and Lana had reached the depot where the train lay abandoned. As they sent the horse on its way, a group of small boats were hurriedly casting off in the port below. The placement of the depot gave them a good view of the activity as it unfolded beneath them.

Pinter cursed under his breath: "Damn. This is a serious operation."

"What are they doing? That's a hell of a lot of stuff to be taking across to the island."

"I don't know, but it can't be good." He nodded in the direction of the dock as he spotted Chaucer being led to a boat. "There he is. The snake. I hope they're paying him well."

Chaucer seemed to be on top of the world. Shakespeare followed behind, looking considerably less enthusiastic.

"Do you think he's having second thoughts?" whispered Lana.

"I'm almost certain." Pinter looked across the water. The island lay far off in the distance, barely visible as a shroud of fog hid it almost entirely from view. He pulled out the parchment he'd retrieved in Wales and consulted it: "That must be where we're headed, where the ceremony is taking place."

"The ceremony?"

Pinter's voice was grave as he replied: "Chaucer was right after all. They're planning a resurrection. They're trying to bring back the Tuatha De. Now that they have all the sacred objects, I suppose they need the power of the Isle of the Tuatha De to triangulate the signal to the divine. That's if we wanted to get technical about this of course. They probably see it as more of a case of aligning the necessary pieces."

"That's a myth, Roop. Just a *myth*! Even my father doesn't believe it and he found that Sword, for crying out loud!"

"Usually I'd be inclined to agree with your father. But if these chaps are as serious as we think they are then we have to try and be just as serious. Besides," he sighed heavily, "there was something strange about each of those artifacts. Something that didn't feel quite right. I don't want to say it, but I'm starting to worry that maybe there's something to this whole thing after all."

She rolled her eyes: "Then what do you propose we do, Roop? Go after them?"

Pinter nodded to a motorboat that lay moored nearby, not in use by the small army on the docks and conveniently hidden from sight by the shape of the wharf. "I wonder if you can read my mind, sometimes."

"It helps."

"We have no choice. If there's any way we can stop this, and stop them, then we have to try."

"Great idea, but do you even know how to…drive…a boat?"

"*Pilot*. Now would seem like a good time to find out, wouldn't it?" he grinned. "Come on."

Pinter allowed himself a moment more to watch the activity on the dock before they jogged down the path towards it. By now most of the men were in boats in the middle of the sea, but Pinter was cautious about those left behind. The last thing they wanted now was to be seen, and for the whole ordeal to have been for nothing. They ducked behind some oil barrels on the dock as a few feet away from them Shakespeare clambered into a dingy opposite Chaucer and pulled the brim of his safari helmet low.

The sun had disappeared behind thick clouds now. There was a strange feeling in the air.

Weather didn't change that quickly. Not even in Wales.

Bill looked like death warmed up as he motioned for one of the men to cast off, and seeing Shakespeare nervous as the boat drifted out into the rising tide only served to make Pinter nervous too. Part of him really hoped that that this was all a badly calculated shot in the dark. A well funded shot in the dark, with no substance to it.

Two of the men had been left behind, presumably to guard the dock and the train in the off chance that the party would return. Pinter sucked in a breath as one of them wandered over to the barrels and lit a cigarette. The roaring motors of the boats would be enough to cover any noise made by a struggle between them, but both men had rifles and the last thing Pinter wanted to do was start a firefight. He checked the clip of the pistol he'd picked up on the train.

One bullet. Only one chance then, and he didn't really want any more blood on his hands. Killing Roach, purely by accident though it was, was enough for one day. He holstered the gun and peeked out over the top of the barrel.

The other guard was kicking his heels by the side of the dock, looking the other way. Perhaps they'd struck luck. Perhaps these two didn't think much of each other. He'd have to act fast.

The rifle hung loosely from the closest guard's back, and silently Pinter gripped the strap. With all his strength, he dragged the man over the barrels, managing to deliver a devastating blow to the back of his head, knocking him out cold. Sliding the dead-weight out of sight, he slipped the rifle off the man's back and gripped it by the barrel. He crept out of cover and towards the other man.

He was within striking distance when his foot slid on the wet concrete and his work boot scraped loudly. The guard barely had time to register the young man stood behind him before the butt of the gun collided with his skull, knocking him for six and sending him spiraling over the edge of the dock, splashing into the murky water below.

Pinter dropped the rifle and waved at Lana, who ran over to join him at the jetty holding the spare boat. He helped her into the boat, hopping in after her as she took up a seat at the front.

Both kept a watchful eye on the boats ahead of them as they slipped into the mist shrouding the island. The weather was really beginning to turn now, with black storm clouds approaching from nowhere. Lana shivered in the cold, and Pinter pulled his jacket from his shoulder-bag.

Handing it to her, he murmured: "Here we go."

He tugged the ripcord and the engine, to his relief, spluttered reluctantly to life on the second go. Then they were off, bouncing over breakers and plunging headlong into the mist that by now had completely engulfed the mysterious island. Guiding their way were the dotted lights of the other boats, twinkling in the gloom like stars twinkling through clouds. A constellation of danger.

THIRTY-THREE

They beached the boat in an alcove, out of sight from the makeshift dock that had been erected hastily by the troops as they arrived. Satisfied that their boat wouldn't be seen by anyone hanging around the dock, they scrambled up the rocky hills lining the beach. As they reached the plateau above the dock, Pinter caught sight of a group of men heading up the trail and into the trees. Silently, he grabbed Lana and pulled her with him to the undergrowth, into cover and out of danger until the men were far enough away to move safely. Far enough to avoid the worry of a straggler turning around for a moment and catching sight of them.

The island was a strange place – overgrown and impossible. Impossible in so many ways. There was no sign of any life on the island other than the new arrivals – no birds, no insects, no wildlife at all. Mist hung in the air like a thick woolen blanket about them, slowly soaking through their already damp clothes. The humidity was eerie, wetter than a jungle but freezing cold. A wind occasionally whipped through the trees, violently shaking the branches, but all at once would stop and the sky around them would be dead and lifeless.

Certain that they wouldn't be seen, Pinter tugged his hat down low and they crawled out of the undergrowth. By now the dock was completely deserted, so the pair walked down to where the boats lay abandoned and empty. Whatever was being transported had already been removed.

Pinter shrugged as he took in the scene: "I suppose we're too late to cut them off now. They must be heading to the ceremony grounds. Further into the island, I suppose."

"So let's get going."

"In a moment or two. Let them get a good lead on us so that we can follow them without being seen. For the time being..." he pulled his pen-knife from his pocket and flipped it open: "...let's slow these buggers down a little bit."

He sliced the mooring ropes and kicked the first boat out, watching it float away in the current. As Lana stood with crossed arms and a disapproving scowl, he made his way round the dock and cut the rest of the boats free. Eventually the ghostly fleet vanished into the thick fog around them. The scowl vanished too when she caught Pinter's boyish grin: "Don't worry. Our boat is perfectly safe. No-one will find it unless they're looking really hard, and I can't imagine that they will be. We just have to be the first off this island if everything goes to hell. Come on, let's go."

Though he was wrapped up in a thick winter jacket and thicker scarf, Shakespeare couldn't stop shivers running up and down his spine, as though the hairs on his back were taking part in a relay race. He led the convoy as it moved slowly along the mountain path, deeper into the island and with every step deeper into the approaching storm. It seemed that with every pace they took the sun sank further and the night drew closer. He checked his pocket watch – though it was only mid afternoon, with the manner in which the clouds were blocking out the sun by the time they reached the ceremony ground it would seem that night had fallen completely.

Perhaps, he thought morbidly, *we will have seen our last sunset.*

It was a terrifying notion.

He shot a look back along the line, where each of the treasures was being carried gingerly by one, or in the case of the Stone of Fal, two of his men. There seemed to be an aura about them, something noticeably bizarre about the artifacts when they were in close proximity to each other. It seemed to scare his men half to death just looking at them. The hardened warriors kept their eyes trained forward.

Again, that feeling of dread rushed through him.

No amount of money was worth this risk.

He looked at the map. They were nearly there now. One more hill and then they'd be at the meeting place. Then he'd get the answers he was looking for, if he chose to hang around for long enough, that is.

"Well," he said gently to himself, quietly enough so that the men following him couldn't hear, "there's only one way to find out."

Pinter and Lana were close behind when the convoy filed into a circular valley and came to a stop. It was like the floor of a volcano, he noticed, with the enclosed shape surrounding a strange structure that had been constructed from heavy stones. It looked to Pinter as one would imagine Stonehenge in its hey-day, the rocks glistening like marble and the enormous stone stacks perfectly rectangular with no sign of erosion. They skirted up the side of the valley and crouched behind some rubble near the top, which granted them a well-hidden but full view of the activity unfolding below. Some of the men had by now set up a base-camp and were taking a well-deserved rest, while those carrying the objects set them down at the centre of the stone circle.

"Incredible..." he murmured, dipping into academic mode. "Absolutely incredible. Randle was right. A ceremony of rites. Neolithic archaeologists seem to agree that Stonehenge is just a larger example of some of the other burial sites, where the stones support a house-like structure, wherein the bones of the dead would be..."

"...ssh!" Lana hissed as she cut in: "We don't have time for a history lesson Rupert. And keep your voice down!"

"We can't ignore the history Lana...this refutes a theory that was deemed as mad. I could write a PhD on this tomorrow. Just have to keep my fingers crossed that the evidence is still here..."

Lana cut him off once again by putting a finger to his lips.

A group of robed figures appeared from a row of tents just clear of the Henge, on the opposite side to the mercenary camp. For a moment, his mind swept back to the tunnels beneath Hellfire Castle and to the horrific robed creatures, but he shook the thoughts away as Shakespeare advanced to meet them, his carefree swagger now replaced by much more reserved and collected movements.

Pinter wasn't sure whether it was out of respect, or simply a complete and utter deficit of confidence had struck his rival.

Lana took his hand and squeezed it.

"Rupert..." Lana whispered, "...what's going on? Who are this lot? Druids?"

"I don't know," Pinter hissed back. "But I've got a nasty feeling about this. A really nasty feeling."

THIRTY-FOUR

"You have done well."

Shakespeare couldn't tell which of the cloaked figures was speaking, let alone make out their faces beneath their dark hoods. Night had fallen now, or had seemed to. The sun was either asleep or couldn't fight the thick clouds above them, so his men powered up generators to illuminate floodlights surrounding the Henge. Deathly shadows were cast as a result, shrouding the expressions of the Druid Brethren in demonic darkness.

"The Brotherhood is indebted to you, Mr Shakespeare."

"You can pay me now, then. I don't particularly fancy hanging around for the fireworks, so I'd like my salary. Please." He tried his best to keep his confident swagger as he spoke, but was all too aware that he was failing miserably at doing so.

Against these nutcases, though, it was all he had left.

One of the cloaked men brought forward a briefcase. As he handed it over, Shakespeare caught a glimpse of the skeletal fingers wrapped around the handle. They were grey and thin, as if all the skin had fallen away and left only the bone.

He checked the contents, finding a satisfactory volume of notes inside. "I'll make a move, then," he said cheerily as he closed the case.

Shakespeare turned on his heel and quickly strolled away, disappearing from sight. The mercenaries watched him go, some collecting their things to follow. Curiosity seemed to get the better of every single one of them and they began to lean on the Henge or squat down on crates to enjoy the show. Shakespeare wandered off alone.

As two of the Druids began to move the Four Treasures into alignment, Chaucer stood completely still, his mouth open in wonder.

"Four corners of the Earth, reunited..." Pinter murmured. "Something that should never have come to be. Don't move until I say."

"We have to stop it!" Panic was slowly flooding into Lana's eyes.

"We can't, not yet. They have guns. And if the fellows we met in Scotland are anything to go by, the men in the cloaks are even more dangerous than the small army down there."

"We have to do something!"

"There's nothing we can do. The moment things get too hairy, we're leaving."

"So you'll let the world end?"

He turned to her and stared deeply into her eyes, allowing her to see the helplessness in his own. They held a look for a moment. Swallowing deeply, he whispered: "I'm trying to think of something. Just trust me."

It was impossible. All of it was impossible. How could

he even begin to formulate a plan, let alone put it into motion? There had to be something he could do, but at the same time his sense of wonder overwhelmed him. Morbid as it was, he wanted to see what happened. He pulled Lana close and kissed her forehead.

"I'll think of something. I promise."

She nodded, and they both turned to look at the ceremony, watching intently as Chaucer moved closer to the treasures. The four artifacts were now arranged in a square at the centre of the Henge, creating symmetry to the whole layout. The Druids then began to congregate, creating a circle around the treasures and blocking Chaucer's view.

There came a low chanting - syllables forming a language that even as a linguistics student Pinter couldn't place. "Must be ancient Celtic," he mused, half to himself and half to Lana. "No-one's heard this in thousands of years. We're lucky."

"Oh, yes..." she muttered, sarcasm ripe as her voice trembled. "Very lucky indeed."

The chanting grew louder, echoing through the valley and reverberating to a level that was nearly deafening. The mercenaries, who seemed to have lost any sense of direction with the departure of Shakespeare, all rose to their feet in wonder, some lighting cigarettes to calm their nerves. Others loaded and re-loaded their guns, as if they hoped that their weapons would protect them if something went wrong. Others still watched on with amused interest as the Druid cloaks began to whirl and flow in time with the chants as they increased in intensity.

Wind tore through the valley, and Pinter pulled off his hat and stuffed it inside his shirt to prevent himself from losing it.

An ethereal green shimmer came over the Four

Treasures, as though caught in some peculiar magic. Pinter supposed that that was exactly what it was, and he couldn't help but be mesmerised as a column of light started to grow skywards, reaching to the heavens. Gradually, the stones of the Henge began to glow blood red. He saw the mercenaries leaning against them leap off in pain, steam rising from where their bodies had been, as if the stones were on fire. Similar shafts of light began to rise from the Henge itself, and the look of awe he'd been wearing became one of concern.

"What on Earth is that?" Lana called over the intense volume of the chanting.

"No idea! But whatever it is, it's working!"

"Is that good or bad?!"

"I'm not sure!"

"We should go!"

"No!" Pinter couldn't believe he was saying it. "Not yet!"

Chaucer spun round in circles on the spot, trying to take it all in. The lights, the colours. He was right. His life's work was finally validated. Now he'd shown those fools at the Sorbonne. Now his Oxford 'colleagues' would cringe. Now they would bemoan his genius. He was right.

"*C'est incroyable!*" He yelled at the top of his voice. "Oh, Randle, *mon ami*! Tirey! If you could see this now! If you could see how right we were! If you could see our work completed! How wonderful! How extraordinary! How incredible!"

Shakespeare caught sight of the pillars of light as he jogged back to the dock. He stood for a moment, entranced by the beauty, by the raw power. He was tempted to go back and take a proper look for himself.

He'd come this far, he'd earned his right to watch. He turned for a moment to return to the ceremony grounds.

Then he caught himself doing so.

He knew better. Caution was key.

Turning on his heel once again, Shakespeare high-tailed it to the dock.

From their vantage point, Pinter and Lana had to shield their eyes as the light grew to a blinding intensity. The chanting was accompanied by a crash of thunder and a flash of lightning, which tore down through the sky and struck the Four Treasures.

The sky opened, light pouring through the shattered black clouds. Pinter, Lana, Chaucer and the Druids all gazed skywards at the same moment.

Lana and Pinter shared a look.

"That can't be good," he said darkly. "That can't be good at all."

Further fingers of lightning ripped through the splinter in the sky and struck the Henge, radiating electricity around the whole structure. The red glow was tinged for a moment with blue-white - ripples of energy radiating in a complete circle, spinning and hissing and popping. Mercenaries within close radius were struck and with blood-curdling screams fell to the floor, sparks crackling through their bodies as they writhed in pain.

Chaucer jumped in shock – somehow, being inside the Henge had meant that he was unaffected by the lightning, just as the cloaked figures were.

All of a sudden, a deathly silence fell. The Druids ceased their chant and fell to their knees. Pinter and Lana watched wide-eyed as Chaucer cautiously approached the four treasures, stepping closer to the circle of bowing robes. They could hear their hearts beating in their throats.

"What the hell is he doing?" Lana hissed, and Pinter clamped his hand over her mouth.

"Ssh!"

There was a terrible foreboding in the air as Chaucer found himself among the cult. There was total silence for a moment except for the quiet whistling of the wind and the tapping of the Frenchman's footsteps. The eerie glow continued, but seemed almost subdued. Christoph Chaucer looked up into the sky, at the growing void beyond, his eyes wide with wonder.

Then, all at once, a rush of thunder boomed across the valley, forks of lightning like the fingers of the gods shot downwards, and his eyeballs exploded.

He screamed in a mix of terror and agony.

A sound Pinter had never heard before, let alone be able to describe, began to echo from the void. It was as though a divine, yet infernal machine came whirring to life – all at once electronic and earthy, a combination which created the most bizarre noise any of them had ever heard. As the intensity of the noise grew louder, Lana clutched her hands to her ears, a silent scream stifled in her throat. He held her closer, his own eyes wide.

Below them, Chaucer fell to his knees, clawing at his empty eye-sockets, blood leaking through his fingers. They felt as though they were on fire, searing into the back of his skull and melting his brain. He screamed in pain as the concentration of the noise around him grew to a volume that drowned him out completely, and blood began to pour from his ears.

The mercenaries, who until now had been lurking around the site, began to run to safety, but it was far too late. Lightning rushed from the void in masses, hundreds of spikes colliding with the ground and with bodies that were caught mid-run, causing them to burst into flames, screaming and leaping around in terror.

Pinter covered Lana's eyes, pulling her into him so that she could bury her face in his chest. "Don't watch. This can only get worse. Don't watch!"

A huge shaft of lightning shot down from the void and struck Chaucer with a strength that lifted him from the ground and suspended him in mid-air. His body was paralysed in fear, and he floated for a moment, glowing and crackling. His entire body began to spark, lightning radiating out of him.

His terrified screams of repentance were the last things he ever uttered, but even they were lost as he combusted, flames tearing him apart and sending sparks and debris rocketing in every direction.

Lana screamed as she heard the sound of the Frenchman exploding, but the Druids took no notice as the whole world began to spin around them. The light was blinding now, blues and reds and greens flashing and whirling. The generators ruptured and the light-bulbs popped, the floodlights too bursting into flames as everything began to rush skyward in the empyrean light. A chilling scream rocketed from the Stone of Fal, which was now white hot in the light except for a black silhouetted figure that seemed to be stood on top of it. It flickered slowly into existence – arms raised.

The bodies of the mercenaries and charred remains of Christoph Chaucer took flight, racing upwards into the mysterious, rippling void that hung above them. As they flew, the Henge broke free of the ground and shot upwards, followed by the billowing robes of the druids as they ascended.

As Pinter watched, the last thing he saw was the Dagda Cauldron, the very thing that had begun this odyssey, as it vanished into the sky and disappeared into the clouds.

The eerie green glare ceased almost immediately, and with a crash of thunder there was silence. As the clouds reformed to a black shade, a light drizzle began.

There was nothing left but the marks on the ground where the lightning had struck and a few boxes, now burning gently and hissing as rainwater touched the flames. The floodlights, petrified and twisted, collapsed to the ground.

Pinter pulled his hat onto his head, tugging it low as he whistled: "Wow. They're gone then."

Lana slowly lifted her head, her whole body trembling as she took a look: "The world didn't end?"

"No," Pinter smiled. "The world didn't end."

"Where did they go, do you think?"

"Maybe we were all wrong. They weren't trying to bring them back. This point of convergence, where the Tuatha De Danann merged the Four Treasures, must have been where the Druids wanted to ascend to *join* them. The Otherworld wasn't hell or heaven...it was the next world along. We were all wrong."

"So the world didn't end because they succeeded after all?"

"Their success came at a price. Who knows what lay on the other side? But I think we're safe for now. As for the world ending...I guess Chaucer was wrong about that as well."

As if to taunt him, there came a low rumbling and the ground began to shudder. He rolled his eyes.

"Or maybe not." He pulled her to her feet as the tremors became a small earthquake. "It's definitely time to leave!"

THIRTY-FIVE

The world seemed to be crumbling around them as Pinter took Lana by the hand and pulled her back towards the path to the dock. Taking one last look behind them, he saw a huge crack disintegrating the floor of the valley. The jaws of the Earth swallowing up all trace of the Tuatha De Danann.

He shuddered when he realised what that meant for them, and pulled Lana faster as the splinter in the valley grew wider.

They were nearing the dock when it struck them what exactly was happening.

"The island...its...it's sinking!" Lana yelled. "How is that possible?"

"Don't ask me!"

Both pushed themselves onwards as fast as they could, spotting the boat up ahead, right where they'd left it. "We need to get clear quickly, or we'll be sucked under when the island goes down!"

"Optimistic, Roop!"

"The story of my life!" He hopped into the boat and pulled the ripcord, not expecting the first tug to give birth to an opportunity. The second had proved more fruitful the first time they'd set off.

But not this time, it seemed, and he panicked. Helping Lana into the boat, he hoped the engine just needed a kick start, and jumped out, pushing the boat into deeper water. As icy water bit his thighs he heaved with all his might and hauled himself back in.

"Come on!" He yelled at the top of his voice. Again, the ripcord did nothing. Lana's eyes were wide:

"Rupert!"

"I know!" He pulled the cord again.

Come on. Please, he begged. *Just work!*

Nothing.

"This could be close!"

"We don't have time for close!" Lana screamed. "Get this bloody boat moving, Rupert Pinter, or so help me God..."

"Shouting at me won't do anything!" He yelled back as he tugged on the ripcord again, and the engine spluttered to life. He couldn't help but smile as he gunned the throttle, forcing the small boat forward, and feeling every bone-shattering shudder as the craft fought the violent waves. Pinter held his hat down tightly over his head as the wind tried to snatch it from him, and sheltered his eyes with his arm as he did so, fighting off the spray that hit him as they were tossed and flung from side to side in the maelstrom. Rain tore at him from all sides.

He gritted his teeth. *This could be close.*

They hit an enormous breaker, and his heart skipped a beat as he felt certain for a moment they were about to capsize. The boat held, crashing back to the sea with an ear splitting crack. For a moment he thought the hull had been torn in two. Water pooled at his feet, but they weren't sinking. His eyes stung intolerably and he used his drenched sleeve to try and clear his vision.

He heard Lana shriek in terror, but they seemed to have hit a sudden calm section. Oddly though, the boat was moving more slowly than it should have been. Following her eyesight, behind the boat, and emanating from the island as it sank beneath the waves, there appeared an enormous tidal wave.

"Oh, Christ," Pinter muttered. Then, yelling to Lana: "Hold on to something!"

He grabbed a rope as quickly as he could, tying it in as tight a knot as he could muster around the engine. Throwing the end to Lana, he wrapped it around his arm and glanced back at the wave.

It would be on them any second.

He pulled off his hat and stuffed it into his shirt again, then motioned to Lana with the rope: "Wrap that around your arm and hold on tight!"

She nodded, fear flooding her eyes. He winked, a boyish smile forced onto his expression in an attempt to reassure her.

"Well..." he yelled, as the shadow of the wave fell over the boat and the nose pitched downwards in the approaching momentum: "No-one said this would be easy!"

He closed his eyes and felt the world fall away, the sharp sting as cold water consumed them, their bodies being flung about underwater and the teeth-like vice of the rope burning his arm, and finally the boat coming away from beneath him as it vanished beneath the wave.

As he opened his eyes, the glare of late afternoon

sunlight was unbelievable. Though his vision stung, a euphoria swept across his body.

He looked around, noticing that they were still afloat. Lana sat upright, trying her best to fix her soaked, matted hair. She caught him looking at her.

"I hate water."

They laughed, for the first time feeling safe.

The island was gone, and instead behind them the sea stretched out to the horizon. The clouds had lifted, as if they were never there. It was almost as if they'd travelled in time.

Ahead of them lay land. Home.

Pinter sighed: "Some proof of this would have been nice."

"At least Randle and Tirey didn't die in vain. Everything they thought was true."

"Randle never would have made it this far," Pinter grinned, though his words still stung with sadness having to use the past tense. "He hated boats. Really hated them."

She clambered over to him, her clothes sloshing in the water that had pooled in the boat. Sitting beside him, she pulled Pinter's arm around her and rested her head on his shoulder. "I guess we all hate something."

"Surprising, really."

"Very. Well...now what?"

"Let's go home."

They struggled with the engine for a few minutes before accepting it was really done for. Pinter unhooked an oar and began rowing them slowly back to civilisation as the island sank further beneath the waves and the Tuatha De Danann further into legend.

THIRTY-SIX

Oxford had a post-winter glow in late February that year, and as the congregation around the coffin removed their overcoats, Pinter felt that perhaps the gods were smiling on his professor as they committed his body to the soil.

Randle's funeral was a subdued affair, attended by a core collection of academic figures, Oxford faculty and former students. Small talk was mostly talking-shop. For a law student like Lana, it was difficult to mingle inconspicuously with the tweed-wearing attendees, but her radiance and beauty at the ceremony meant that she was destined to be conspicuous.

Pinter grinned, enjoying her company, but also the fact that she was with him. It was fun showing her off.

As the priest concluded, Pinter found ample time to throw a hunting hat in on top of the coffin as it was lowered into the ground. It had been returned by post, rescued as it floated downstream by one of the team sent to Wales by the University during their investigation.

It seemed fitting that Pinter should be the one to return it to its owner.

Though he had no refutable proof of what had happened, the University had been gracious enough to give Pinter some breathing space for the whole affair. Thankfully Harding-Rosenthal, in a rare good mood, had commended Pinter for a job well done, with a relaxed warning that he should stay out of trouble, and a referral to Dr Peter Aird for induction into the History Undergraduate scheme.

Everything was coming up roses.

Lana rejoined him, the eyes of Pinter's classmates following her as she did so. She grinned: "The history lot are friendly."

"A pretty girl like you? You could have your pick of them."

She giggled. "Never mind. Besides, I know which one I'd choose." Slipping her arm through his, they followed the crowd as it dispersed. "My father wants to know when you'll be finishing the conversation you started with him?"

"How much scotch will he force feed me?"

"Probably far too much," she grinned. "Come on."

They headed towards the line of cars that were waiting at the gates of the cemetery, and as soon as they were out on the main road she pulled him to her and landed a passionate kiss on his lips, wrapping her arms around his neck. He returned it, drinking in the moment.

When she pulled away, he couldn't help but smile again and watch as she ducked into a car as he held the door.

"My father is expecting you for dinner tonight. He doesn't believe my version of events, so I'll need you to confirm them. Once a skeptic, always a skeptic. How does half past seven sound?"

"Wonderful."

"Dinner suits, of course."

"Of course. And canapés in the billiards room?" He teased.

"I'll see you around, Roop," she smiled.

He closed the door and watched the car head off into the distance. The sun continued to shine and it had the makings of a glorious day. Even with all his aches and pains, everything felt right with the world.

There came a shout from behind him as one of the funeral directors jogged his way: "Are you Mr Pinter?"

"Alexander or Rupert?"

"I'm looking for Rupert, I believe."

"That's me."

"I see. You were left this," the short, stout fellow handed him a letter. Randle's handwriting had scrawled his name on the front. "I'm sorry for your loss."

The man slunk away and Pinter gently tore open the envelope, pulling out the letter and reading it as he walked:

My dear friend,

If you are reading this then our last adventure has come to an end, but it would seem that I am now on the greatest adventure possible — a voyage into the unknown. Do not grieve for me. You have far too much to do before you follow me on this trail.

Your father was a great man. One of the best I've ever known. Before he died he made two things very clear — that despite the fact that he was a doctor of medicine, he was useless in the mornings, and also that he put you above and beyond everything else in his life. Your father was an old-fashioned man, and didn't know how to show it, but approved of everything you ever did. If you can come to terms with his passing and accept that he was, and always will be, truly proud of you, then there is nothing left to hold you back.

You were the son I never had. Make me proud, just as you already have your father.

Yours,
Geoffrey Randle

Rupert Pinter folded the letter silently and placed it inside his suit-jacket pocket. For a moment he wanted to be alone.

Shaking off the strange mix of sadness and happiness he slung his overcoat onto his shoulder and started on the long walk back to his flat. In any other circumstance he would have hailed one of the passing taxis, but the weather was far too good to waste.

His mind went to Shakespeare as he walked, only fleetingly, but for long enough to wonder where on Earth the man went. His body hadn't been among those flung into the void – he'd left long before things got nasty.

Which certainly couldn't be a good thing.

Pinter shook his head, guessing that it wouldn't be the last he'd see of Bill Shakespeare. He laughed, then murmured: "Well, I suppose life is cyclical..." to no-one in particular.

As he watched a bird curling upwards, his thoughts were on Randle once more, and what the old man had said as he died.

'If you must play, decide on three things at the start: the rules of the game, the stakes, and the quitting time.'

An appropriate adage.

Perhaps even words to live by.

He quickened his pace, and the bird rushed up into the clouds, disappearing out of sight.

EPILOGUE

Marrakesh, Morocco
ONE YEAR LATER

The smell of orange and spice, sweat and blood, dirt and animals hung in the air like a blanket. Steam rose from seared lamb and chicken roasting on wheeled kitchens, mixing with the cigarette smoke of seated Arabs leering from their stalls, rotting teeth hanging the dark abyss of their grins.

It was a hundred degrees outside but Bill Shakespeare shivered as a breeze swept through the souk. Goose-bumps raced skyward, through the thin layer of sweat that covered his body.

He drew a handkerchief from the breast pocket of his white linen suit and wiped his brow, his eyes open as he did so, watching, daring the pickpockets who lurked in shadows to make their approach. He hated Marrakesh, but some destinations were necessary evils. Fortunately he had found consolation in the endless supply of Berber whiskey.

He returned the handkerchief and snapped a cigarette case open with a force that attracted the *dirham* hungry eyes of the nearest shopkeeper.

The smoke was cheap but delicious, and Shakespeare drank the blue haze in like a fine wine as his grey eyes darted around him for the entrance to the cafe he'd come to find.

It was well hidden. He had to hand it to his potential client – if he didn't like the company it wasn't difficult for a man to vanish in the labyrinth of cheap teapot sellers and carpet peddlers.

A dark thought wandered into his consciousness. The ease in getting rid of someone without a trace and without evidence. How many Arabs would report the death of a white man in this maelstrom?

At last, the entrance to the back-alley shisha cafe appeared, shrouded in mist and almost hidden by a tattered, ash-stained rug. The place had seen better times. Shakespeare brushed his way through and into a small chamber. It was barely a cafe at all – windowless, dark, dingy. The purple smoke of hashish and shisha mixing into a potent brew blocked the ceiling from view completely. His head swam for a moment.

A collection of Arabs huddled around tiny tables supporting pipes that looked too heavy for their weight to be held. A couple of blood-shot white eyes darted in his direction, but the accusing looks quickly retreated into their dark turbans.

A hand grasped his back, and Shakespeare could feel his heart beating against his wallet.

"*Salam*, Mr Shakespeare. You are not an inconspicuous man. I trust you had no trouble finding us?"

Shakespeare turned slowly to face the voice, and found at his side a short, rotund man with a cracked nose and crooked teeth. His eyes were black in the dim light of the cafe, and the only features highlighted in the yellow-orange light were the numerous scars that mapped his face.

"I find that impressions are best made once, Hamid. This is a charming place, though I had to pay a man to lead me to the correct souk."

"Everyone in Marrakesh is a salesman, Mr Shakespeare. Even those with nothing to sell." Hamid motioned to an empty space on the floor: "Please?"

Shakespeare took a seat on a rug beside a table as a thinner Arab appeared like a ghost from one of the dark corners of the building and set up a pipe. The actions were quick, and within moments Hamid had collapsed onto the floor beside him, one of the distributors in his mouth. It remained there as he talked, smoke hissing between his teeth: "You understand why I invited you to see me, yes?"

"Barely. Though I understand you have some need for my services?"

"You have made quite a reputation for yourself." He offered the pipe.

"One I'd prefer to keep," Shakespeare added, taking the pipe and sucking deeply. As he replied, a thick plume of white smoke shrouded him: "So you'll understand that I'll need to make my fee perfectly clear."

"You will be paid well."

"It was discussed when I was in Paris last year that preparations would have to be made. I trust that this is the case?"

"Your colleague made it…imperative."

"She is persuasive."

"She is a beautiful woman."

"She is…" Shakespeare murmured. The thought of her

danced across his eyes for a moment. He took one last drag on the shisha pipe and handed the distributor back to the squat Arab.

"Everything is in place," Hamid cut in. We simply need your…commitment…to the project."

"For something I know little about, you seem to have a lot of confidence in my 'commitment.'"

"I had heard that you were the best. I only hire the best."

"Well then, Hamid…" Shakespeare leant forward conspiratorially. 'What is it that I can do for you?"

Hamid smiled, warming to his game. He motioned to one of the attendants and in clipped Arabic ordered a pot of mint tea. He leant in closer, sucking on the pipe and letting the smoke escape in extravagant plumes.

"Tell me, Mr Shakespeare…what do you know of the Knights Templar?"

HISTORICAL NOTES

THE TUATHA DE DANANN

Though fictionalized for the purposes of this novel, the Tuatha Dé Danann ("peoples of the goddess Danu") are a race of people in Irish mythology. In the invasions tradition which begins with the *Lebor Gabála Érenn*, they are the fifth group to settle Ireland, conquering the island from the Fir Bolg. The Tuatha Dé Danann are thought to derive from the pre-Christian deities of Ireland.

When the surviving stories were written, Ireland had been Christian for centuries, and the Tuatha Dé were represented as mortal kings, queens and heroes of the distant past; however there are many clues to their former divine status. A poem in the *Book of Leinster* lists many of them, but ends "Although [the author] enumerates them, he does not worship them." The Dagda's name is interpreted in medieval texts as "the good god."

Even after they are displaced as the rulers of Ireland

prominent characters in the legend, such as Lugh, the Morrígan, Aengus and Manannán mac Lir appear in stories set centuries later, showing all the signs of immortality, with many parallels across the Celtic world.

FRANCIS DASHWOOD AND THE HELLFIRE CLUB

Dashwood was born in London and educated at Eton College. He was too young to have been a member of the very first Hellfire Club founded by the Duke of Wharton in 1719 and disbanded in 1721 but he and the Earl of Sandwich are alleged to have been members of a Hellfire Club that met at the George and Vulture Inn throughout the 1730s.

By 1732 he had formed a dining club called the *Society of Dilettanti* which had around 40 charter members - some of whom are likely to have been members of Wharton's original club. Dashwood then leased Medmenham Abbey on the Thames in 1751 and had it rebuilt by the architect Nicholas Revett in the style of the 18th century Gothic revival. The first meeting of the group is known, facetiously, as *Brotherhood of St. Francis of Wycombe, Order of Knights of West Wycombe* - the Hellfire name did not appear until much later. It was held at Sir Francis' family home in West Wycombe, but the initial meeting was something of a failure and the club subsequently moved their meetings to Medmenham Abbey, about 6 miles from West Wycombe, where they called themselves the *Monks of Medmenham*.

As far as his activities in the Hellfire Club are concerned, he was in his day widely regarded as being involved in devil worship. What really occurred in these meetings we will never know, but underneath the Abbey, Dashwood had a series of caves carved out from an existing one. It was, however, decorated with mythological themes, phallic symbols and other items of a sexual nature.

THE R101 AIRSHIP

While most know of the *Hindenburg*, infamous for the disaster that put an end to airship use as a viable commercial system of international travel, the *R101* was one of a pair of British rigid airships completed in 1929 as part of a British government programme to develop civil airships capable of service on long-distance routes within the British Empire. Designed and built by an Air Ministry-appointed team, it was the world's largest flying craft and it was not surpassed until the *Hindenburg* flew five years later.

After trial flights and subsequent modifications to increase lifting capacity it crashed on the 5th October 1930 in France during its maiden overseas voyage, resulting in the deaths of 48 of the 54 people on board. The crash of R101 effectively ended British airship development, and was one of the worst airship accidents of the 1930s. The loss of life was greater than in the *Hindenburg* disaster of 1937 and was second only to the USS *Akron* crash in 1933.

ABOUT THE AUTHOR

Robert NC Thomas, born and bred in Cardiff, Wales, is a part-time historian and armchair adventurer. His real-life adventures have taken him across the world from China to Peru. He lives and works in Cardiff after graduating with a degree in History from Cardiff University, and he refuses to be a grown-up.

RUPERT PINTER AND THE CURSE OF THE TUATHA DE DANANN